BEING HERE
by Jennifer Lynn

BEING HERE
by
Jennifer Lynn
Copyright © Jennifer Lynn 2017
Cover Copyright © Dawn Leslie Lenz 2017
Published by Craig Na Dun
(An Imprint of Ravenswood Publishing)

CRAIGH NA DUN

Names, characters and incidents depicted in this book are products of the author's imagination, or are used fictitiously. Any resemblance to actual events, locales, organizations, or persons, living or dead, is entirely coincidental and beyond the intent of the author or the publisher.

All rights reserved. No part of this book may be reproduced or transmitted in any form or by any means whatsoever, including photocopying, recording or by any information storage and retrieval system, without written permission from the publisher and/or author.

Ravenswood Publishing
1275 Baptist Chapel Rd.
Autryville, NC 28318
http://www.ravenswoodpublishing.com

Printed in the U.S.A.

ISBN-13: 978-0692837030
ISBN-10: 0692837035

DEDICATION

For Love, in the positive polarity.

AUTHOR'S NOTE
THE MAGIC OF STORY

Before DVDs, films and even radio... back in times when people lived more closely to the earth, lived more in harmony with the ebbing and flowing rhythms of life... at night when the sun set to restore evening darkness, people would gather around the fire.

In circles they gathered to share warmth, food and stories... of the day now gone... of people long cherished and remembered... of life in its unfolding... stories of wisdom that helped them to remember the Sacred Ways.

Tapping into the magic of that ancient tradition, I offer you book one of the story of Bree MacLeod... woman, *Bean feasa*, shaman... living her life – in This World and the Otherworld – in Love, in the Grace of the Goddess and in the magic of the Mystery.

Beannachtaí... Blessings...

CHAPTER ONE

Seattle-Tacoma International Airport was the last place — in This World or the Otherworld — Bree MacLeod wanted to be. Nevertheless, the steel-grey wall of rain falling outside the terminal window insisted she was here. That and the school of brass salmon etched into the floor beneath her feet. Bree took a deep breath and exhaled slowly. *Welcome back*, the salmon seemed to whisper.

Before Bree's tired eyes the brass salmon blurred as memory rose into vision. *"Why do they all swim away, Papa?"*

She was a girl again, hopping from salmon to salmon, tracking their Otherworldly migration upstream, along the floor. Diving to grasp the wriggling, ethereal shapes, she peeked hopefully into her tiny hands only to find them empty, cold and wet. She heard the resonant chuckle of her father – so young and full of life in the vision – and wondered... did he know then for Bree the salmon were real?

Bree's world shook. A mumbled "Sorry" drifted in the passenger's hurried wake as she shifted her messenger bag back to a comfortable position on her shoulder.

So many people... Bree didn't like crowds. After the quiet, misty peace of the Irish countryside, SeaTac airport screamed like a rock concert. People spilling in endless waves around her, Bree looked down at her feet trying to conjure the green grass of the Curragh. Instead, her Salmon Ally blinked back at her. Hovering with the brass school, Salmon waited patiently, watching her, reminding her.

"Okay Salmon," Bree whispered. "I'm here, in Seattle. Guide me with your Wisdom, shelter me in Grace, and show me the way."

To her inner eye, the salmon beneath her winked delightedly and swam ahead. With a sigh, Bree followed her Salmon Ally out of the terminal and headed toward baggage claim.

CHAPTER TWO

The hospital room was long and narrow. The drapes had been left open, but no matter. The grey outside would hardly disturb the sleeping patient.

"Emily..."

The name of her aunt escaped as a whisper, an echo of the shock coursing through Bree as she stood before that bed. If she hadn't known it was her aunt... the withered, grey-haired thing in the bed looked nothing like the woman she knew and loved. Except for the nose. The nose was unmistakable.

But it was Emily's hands that awakened memory inside Bree. Now shrunken and frail, those hands had once held strength, wisdom and courage. They had taught Bree to love the earth, to till soil, to pull weeds from garden beds and to clip herbs with tender care and gratitude for life. They were agile, too, spinning wool into yarn, untangling with ease the mess that Bree's hands had spun. Bree could still feel the rhythm of those hands in her bones... twist, twist, pull... twist, twist, pull... twist, twist, pull...

Emily had been like a mother to Bree; yet, rather painfully, they looked nothing alike. Sinewy and petite, Emily was tiny compared to Bree, who looked more like her rugby-playing father than her elegant mother. Bree had envied Emily's trimness and her red hair. It blazed with a fire more ancient than words. Raven-black hair spilled over Bree's broad shoulders, proclaiming the truth of her mother's blood. *Black Irish, Raven Child* they had called her in college. Then Bree had laughed at the nickname. Now she only wondered, could they have known?

The touch of a curl twirling in her fingers awakened another memory. Emily had taught Bree to braid her hair. Twist, twist, pull... twist, twist, pull... twist, twist, pull...

"What are you doing here?"

The nurse's voice drew Bree back to the bedside. Emily's hands lay unmoving against the white sheets. Despite the impatience of the nurse bristling beside her, Bree could not remove her eyes from those hands.

"I said, *what* are you doing here?"

The force of the nurse's demand struck Bree from behind, breaking the hold of Emily's hands upon her. Bree gasped slightly, then turned to face the nurse.

"I... um..." Bree stammered, distracted by the sudden shift in focus. "I... I was hoping to see Emily's chart."

"Charts are for doctors," replied the nurse.

Bree frowned. "I am a doctor." Even to Bree, her voice sounded tired and small.

The nurse ran her eyes disapprovingly over Bree and cocked one eyebrow. "*You're* a doctor?" The nurse's tone conveyed the depths of her doubt as her eyes swept once more over Bree only to pronounce her not only lacking, but utterly unbelievable.

Not exactly hospital wear, Bree thought, her hands moving to smooth the wrinkles of travel from her stale jeans and cotton shirt. They had been clean and fresh when she left Shannon.

How long ago was that now? Bree tried to tally the hours mentally. After two cancelled connections and an unexpected overnight in Newark, she had been on the road, what, thirty-four hours? Or was it thirty-six? She was too tired to be sure. She had left Shannon yesterday morning; that much she knew for certain.

Shannon... Ireland... the Curragh... quiet... refuge... *No*, Bree thought, *no... not now.*

"I came straight from the airport," Bree offered in explanation.

The nurse lifted a hand to her hip.

"I flew in by request of the family, to consult," Bree countered the unyielding nurse. "And, yes, I am a doctor."

The nurse just stood there.

Bree began to doubt the odds of the woman being at all helpful. Reaching through fatigue for her mantle of authority, she tried again. "Dr. Walters, Emily's Attending, is expecting me."

"*Is* he now," the nurse drawled, turning to leave the room. Suddenly, Bree thought, the room tasted awfully sour.

"He is indeed." Dr. Walters, a tall, trim man with graying temples, stood outlined in the doorway. His stark white lab coat tried to offset the gloom of the room, but to no avail. With a frown at the exiting nurse, the doctor stepped forward, hand extended. "I'm Dr. Walters, Emily's Attending. You must be Dr. MacLeod."

He was smiling genuinely, Bree noticed. Extending her own hand, she returned the smile and the pleasant greeting, noting inwardly that her cousine Rose must have given him the usual background, conveniently omitting her *other* credentials.

"Rose speaks very highly of you," Dr. Walters offered. "She said you practice in St. Louis?"

"Yes," Bree nodded. "I have a private practice in the Clayton area."

Let him hear what he needs to hear, Bree thought as she continued answering his polite questions. She was a doctor, a specialist in internal medicine actually. But she rarely practiced that medicine anymore. Nor did Rose fly her halfway across the world for that. No, it was her *other* gifts Emily needed.

They had resurfaced during medical school, those *other* gifts, during her rotation in the ER. She had denied it at first, explained it away as a combination of solid training and excellent diagnostic skills. But over time, people began to comment about Bree's uncanny ability to nail the problem every time.

She just *knew*. Patients would come in, and Bree would take one look and *know*.

Her Chief of Residency was the first to mention it. "They all recover." He had waited for Bree to say something, anything in explanation, but she knew enough to keep quiet. Besides, she was still trying to explain it to herself.

Then she started seeing them, people walking the corridors of the hospital that no one seemed to notice. Except Bree. But when they started visiting her at home, she realized it was time to seek help.

Sensitive, the priest had called her. Hailing from Ireland, he grew up on stories of people who could see and hear "through the Veil." He made it sound so normal. And he had reminded her... "Were you uncanny as a child? Did you see and hear things that others could not?"

Like the salmon slipping through her fingers in SeaTac airport, Bree thought. And afternoon tea with the herb spirits in Emily's garden. Or the nighttime stories with her deceased mother.

"My blood flows within you," her mother would whisper to Bree from the Otherworld. "Some day you will have to embrace the gift that blood brings."

The priest was kind to Bree. He even gave her the name of someone who could answer her questions more thoroughly. But it was Emily who had responded. Sensing something was troubling her niece, she had telephoned in the middle of the night.

"You are a *Bean feasa*, a wise woman, a shaman," Emily told the sobbing Bree. "One of the *Aes Dána*, the Gifted who can see and move through the Veil."

Veil? What veil, Bree wanted to know.

Her aunt, patient and tender as always, explained. "The Veil between the world of physical reality and the world of soul. You are a bridge between the two, as were your mother and grandmother before you."

Bree's mind wanted to panic, to run in circles screaming. But her body simply exhaled, recognizing the truth of Emily's words.

"The women of our bloodline are the daughters of Bríghid, the Celtic goddess of the sacred flame. It is Her blood that gifts you, that calls your soul to the Work. While Her blood flows through us all, only the first-born daughter carries the fullness of Her Gift."

Her heart had pounded. In Bree's inner vision, she watched her lineage etch itself in opalescent trees that blazed against the darkness. Tracking through generations, she followed the names from first-born daughter to first-born daughter. Her eyes widening slightly, Bree saw the truth just as Emily spoke it.

"Bree, you are the first-born daughter."

Bree shook her head slowly in the darkness. *I don't understand,* her mind insisted.

"*Yes you do,*" a voice – feminine, ancient, loving – answered within her.

"That is all I can tell you," Emily had said in the end. "If you want to know more, you will need to ask your mother. She can tell you what you need to know."

"But..." Bree had stammered, her mind reeling to process what Emily had told her. "But, she is dead."

Dr. Walters placed something in Bree's hands. She shook herself slightly to bring her focus back to the hospital room. She was tired. She really should sleep, but Emily needed her.

Bree centered her awareness on Dr. Walters' voice, using it like an Otherworldly rope to pull herself back to the present.

"Everything should be there, in Emily's chart, but if you need anything, please don't hesitate to ask. I'll let the nurse know to offer you all assistance."

Dr. Walters started toward the door. "I'm not sure what more you can do, Doctor. Emily has been seen by the best of our staff. But since Rose thinks you can help, well…" With a nod he disappeared through the doorway, leaving the bitter tang of doubt trailing with his cologne.

"At least he was helpful," Bree muttered to herself.

JENNIFER LYNN

CHAPTER THREE

Bree sank into the small sofa that filled the far end of the hospital room, grateful to be off her feet. Her body ached with fatigue. Traveling west always seemed more difficult. She closed her eyes and rested her head in her hand. A nap would feel so good... but Salmon was there, dancing in the darkness of vision, reminding her.

"Emily needs you."

Salmon's words echoed anew within Bree and she frowned. Rose had spoken those very same words when she had telephoned one week ago. The sorrow in her cousine's voice had torn at Bree's heart. Of course she had agreed to offer what healing she could to Emily.

With Rose's blessing, Bree had begun with the usual diagnostic journey to see if Emily welcomed her assistance and, if so, how best to proceed.

"Emily needs you," Salmon had confirmed. *"You need each other. Go to her, Raven Child. Only there can healing flow."*

Go to her... the words, the very idea had shocked Bree breathless.

Why, Bree had challenged her Ally. Why did she need to board an airplane and physically go to Seattle to help Emily? She had helped so many others in her healing work as a *Bean feasa* without travelling physically to their locations. Bree had made herself a promise never to return to Seattle. Surely she could offer the needed healing for Emily from the peace and sanctuary of her cottage in Ireland.

But Salmon had insisted. *"Go to her, Raven Child."*

Uncomfortable with Salmon's advice, Bree had summoned her Council of Allies, the group of Otherworldly beings responsible for teaching, supporting and guiding Bree in her soul's Work. Bree knew Salmon well, she trusted his advice, but this situation required something more. Before she set foot in Seattle, she needed to hear the wisdom of her Council and receive the blessing of those who knew her soul and its purpose the best.

They had gathered in the Otherworld as always, nestled in the shelter of the ancient grove. With the Oak Spirits bearing silent witness, Bree had stepped bare-footed onto the centuries-old moss and walked the circle of her Allies. One by one her Allies had spoken… *"Go to her, Raven Child. Only there can healing flow."*

"Okay, Allies," Bree spoke into the gloom of Emily's hospital room. "I am here. Salmon, show me the way."

Bree sighed. Keeping her eyes closed, she lifted her head and tucked her feet up underneath her. Resting both hands on the printout of Emily's chart in her lap, Bree drew a centering breath. As Salmon continued to swim in her vision, she called quietly to the *Airds* – north, east, south, west and center – summoning a circle of enfolding protection. Then, with an exhale she followed Salmon through the Veil…

...Laughter, joyous and flowing, ripples and cascades to fill Bree's world. Welcoming the wisdom that Salmon would reveal to her, Bree opens her eyes to the Otherworld.

Light, golden and incandescent, caresses life all around. Glorious streaks of blue, crimson and gold sway among a sea of green, as endless waves of wildflowers ripple and shimmer, dancing in an Otherworldly breeze.

Bathed in that light, a woman turns circles, arms spread wide, red hair blazing in the kiss of the sun. Strong and supple, her hands glide, palms cupped skyward to drink in the radiance. Her delight rolls with the waves as peals of laughter, rippling and flowing with the pulse of life. And that dancing sea sings back to her, in streaks of gold, crimson and blue, in peals of pulsating Love.

Salmon nods his silent confirmation, but Bree would know that red hair anywhere. "She dances," his voice thrums unspoken in her mind. "She dances neither fully here nor there."

Rippling laughter rings through Bree's awareness and blurs the waters of vision. Light fading to emptiness, Bree rises and stretches her arms to soar, her black feathers rustling on Otherworldly currents. Another awareness presses into her, familiar, soothing.

"Crrruck!" Her Raven Ally calls. "Come back, Raven Child. Come back and let Emily choose."

Breathing deeply, returning back to physical reality, Bree opened her eyes to see the printout of Emily's chart resting patiently in her lap. She knew what it would say. Patient non-responsive, pathology results negative, no obvious trauma, idiopathic coma.

She opened it and read it anyway.

CHAPTER FOUR

Bree closed the folder containing her aunt's chart as the door to Emily's room opened. *Another scolding*, she thought with a sigh, betting to find the nurse on the other side of the door. But, no, she realized as the door opened wider, the energy was wrong. This energy was earthy, strong but tender, and *familiar*.

"I trust I am not interrupting…"

A woman's smiling face peeked around the edge of the open door. The woman's hazel eyes danced with merriment.

"Rose!"

Bree scrambled to avoid dropping the copy of Emily's chart as she stood eagerly to greet her cousine. Rose laughed and swept Bree into a warm, swaying embrace.

They were equal in stature, both unusually strong and broad-shouldered, although Rose stood almost a head taller than Bree. A head, Bree had often rued, that blazed defiantly with cascades of Emily's red hair. Well, naturally. Rose was, after all, Emily's daughter. The red hair proclaimed it true… the hair and the nose.

"I figured you would come straight from the airport. I'm so sorry I wasn't there to pick you up." Rose said, stepping back to get a good view of her cousine.

"It's all right," Bree nodded. "Besides, this wasn't exactly the arrival time we had planned."

"Too true." Bree watched a smile dance across Rose's face – the delight in seeing her cousine clear – then fade into a look of concern. "But Bree... cousine, you look exhausted."

"Actually, I am," Bree had to admit. She never could sleep on planes. Too many people with too many emotions packed too tightly into a pressurized space... a deadly combination for any empath, much less for one of her training and sensitivity.

"Come, let me take you home." Rose herded Bree toward the door.

"But, Emily..." Bree countered, turning to look back over her shoulder at the withered form in the bed.

Bree was no longer moving. A glance at her cousine explained the change. Like Bree, Rose had turned to face her mother.

Bree watched as the eyes so recently dancing with delight drowned in unspoken sorrow. Rose seemed frozen, gazing painfully at the still form of her mother. Conscious of her cousine's unspoken despair, Bree slipped her arm around Rose in silent support. With a bleak smile, Rose squeezed Bree's hand.

"I would have helped her myself..." Rose began, but her voice disappeared into silence.

"I know." It was all Bree could say. They had said everything else already.

"She won't let me in," Rose had explained when she had telephoned Bree in Ireland. "I keep trying to reach her, to offer what assistance I can, but the journey just ends. Every time. I step into the Otherworld, call to her and everything goes blank."

"Maybe she doesn't want help. Maybe she wants to sort this – whatever this is – on her own."

That was a stretch and Bree had known it, even as she spoke the words. But Rose's grief chaffed painfully in Bree's awareness. She wanted so to help ease her cousine's anguish, to rebuke the unspoken question: *Am I failing her?*

"Perhaps," Rose had countered. "Or maybe she is waiting for you."

The two women had agreed. Bree would begin with a journey to assess and ask what, if any, healing could be offered to Emily, for her highest good and honoring her soul's choice. If healing were allowed, Bree would seek guidance on how best to affect that healing. Then she would report back to Rose.

Neither of them had expected Bree to say she was coming to Seattle. Yet, here she was, in Emily's hospital room, standing next to Rose.

"Yes," Rose breathed, "she does need you." Then her sorrow dispersed in a ray of returning delight. "But, if I know you, cousine, you have done what little you can for now. Hmmm?" Rose cocked an eyebrow teasingly and Bree laughed at the familiarity of the gesture. "Besides," Rose persisted, "my house is much more appropriate for that sort of Work, now, isn't it?"

Bree could hardly argue with that.

Rose maintained her own level of mystical practice and kept a wonderful space for Working. On several occasions since Bree had escaped to St. Louis, the two women had Worked together remotely, offering healing to people in crisis. Most of those times Rose had found herself in waters too deep for her shamanic training and had contacted Bree for assistance completing the Work. But Bree also remembered a few times when she had reached out to Rose, needing a Second to support her in holding space or completing simultaneous healing work in the Otherworld.

Rose was a skilled practitioner, no doubt. But, as the first-born daughter of a *second*-born daughter of the bloodline, Rose was free to choose. While Bree was pulled more and more deeply into shamanic healing techniques, soul matrices and energy medicine, Rose chose the path of motherhood and cultivated a family. And as a dedicated mother, she placed the good of her family over the deepening of her mystical practice. In the end, Bree's calling as a first-born daughter of Bríghid brought her skills and practice into the public eye, while Rose practiced quietly, privately with as little public proclamation as possible.

I might have made the same choice, had I dared to stay, Bree thought quietly, standing beside Rose and gazing at Emily. Dropping her eyes to the floor, Bree frowned inwardly. *No... no, that could never have happened.*

"Besides," Rose whispered conspiratorially, "if we leave now, we can avoid seeing *you-know-who*."

"You mean, he drives in to see her?" Surprise flowed openly in Bree's voice.

"Yup, at 4 pm sharp, so…" Rose flashed Bree a view of the clock. 3:15 pm blinked into view.

"By your lead…" Bree half bowed, ready to be anywhere but where her uncle might be.

JENNIFER LYNN

CHAPTER FIVE

"The room is pretty much the same as the last time you stayed here." Rose placed a set of clean towels on top of the dresser in her guest bedroom. "Actually, I think you *were* the last person in this room."

Bree caught the ironic smile that flitted across her cousine's face and sighed inwardly at the familiar jest. They had been close, like sisters, before Bree had left Seattle and the distance had been hard for Rose to accept. Rose often invited her to visit, but Bree repeatedly declined.

Once, and only once, Rose had been successful in drawing Bree back to Seattle. Three years after her marriage, Rose gave birth to her first child, a daughter. Bree was in Victoria, British Columbia, at the time, teaching at the local medical college and mentoring clients, local students of the Mystery. Unaware of the beautiful birthing unfolding just across the Strait of Juan de Fuca, Bree finished the semester and withdrew to Salt Spring Island for a month of silence, meditation and spiritual questing.

The monks who ran the retreat center supported Bree in her month of isolation. The path to her cabin was roped off and marked with a sign that read "Silence : Seclusion In Progress." Each morning, the monks delivered a tray of fresh food and water to Bree. Rather than carry it to her and disturb her silence, the monks left the tray in a special cooler along the path to her cabin. Every day Bree walked to the cooler, gathered the tray of fresh items and deposited the empty tray from the previous day as a sign that she was well. This exchange of trays was her only form of communication with the outside world.

Bree agreed with the strict policy of no contact from the outside world during a period of seclusion. She even looked forward to it, every time she withdrew into retreat. Settling into that deep level of quiet, Bree finally breathed free from the demands of the energies and emotions of others, if only for a little while.

The card on the tray had screamed its presence. Bree sensed the change in the energetic pattern of her seclusion as a frisson of disruption rising with the sun. She spent the morning sitting with the unexpected shift, just allowing it to be there. She thought that in honoring it, the disrupting energy might abate. Instead, it grew increasingly uncomfortable. With a sigh, Bree uncurled her legs, bowed to her meditation cushion and walked to the cooler.

The message had been simple and to the point. "Rose called. Please come and name her daughter."

As the current first-born daughter of Bríghid, Bree acted as *Bean feasa* for the women of her bloodline. Conducting the naming ceremony was part of this calling. Reading the message, Bree had sensed in her blood the call to go. The next day, a week earlier than planned, she terminated her seclusion and caught the Black Ball ferry to the States.

Bree remembered the gentle rush of power that met her as she stepped barefoot into the center of the family's ritual grove. So much love had flowed, blessing the spirits of that place, Bree and the immediate family members who encircled her. She remembered standing as *Bean feasa* and holding her three-month-old niece in her arms as she called upon Mother Bríghid to shelter this life in its becoming. Ritually merged and flowing with the Love of Bríghid, Bree watched as, through her, Bríghid Herself blessed the child with water, earth and fire – the sacred elements of the goddess. As one, Bríghid and Bree raised the girl to be bathed in the light and called to Moon, Sun and Star to ask for Their blessing as well. While Bríghid kissed the child's brow, Bree spoke aloud the name the goddess had gifted... Fiona.

Even then, Bree had never intended to remain in Seattle. She arrived prepared to conduct the ceremony and never bothered to unpack. In the end, she had stayed in Rose's guestroom for only three days before returning to Victoria. How could she explain that being there hurt too much?

Then and now, that discussion led nowhere useful. Instead, Bree simply smiled. "Come, cousine, I am sure you have more company than that."

"Mmmmm..." Rose muttered, letting the subject drop as she turned down the bed. Lavender blossomed to fill the room and Bree smiled. Emily always scented her sheets in lavender. Rose, it seemed, was keeping the tradition.

"Do you need anything else?" Rose looked around the room, searching for what, if anything, she might have forgotten. "An extra blanket? Or perhaps a Second?"

Bree smiled. *Feels like old times.* "No, cousine, but thank you."

"Are you sure," Rose persisted. "You are planning to Work tonight, aren't you?"

How well her cousine knew her, and why not? They had grown up together, had taken their first steps into the ebbings and flowings of the Otherworld together. They were sisters in everything, except blood. Sometimes Bree had to remind herself that they were born of different mothers.

Bree exhaled deeply, grateful for the steady strength of her cousine beside her. "Yes, cousine, I will Work tonight, but only briefly. We needn't both lose sleep for it."

Rose squinted at Bree, looking at her more deeply than usual. "You are sure?"

Bree laughed, drawing a chuckle from her cousine as well. "Yes, I am sure." Tiny teeth nipped at her awareness and she recognized it as Rose's eagerness to help. "Don't worry," Bree added, "there will be more Work soon enough."

Rose smiled at her and a wave of delight washed over Bree. Standing here in this house, in the company of her cousine, Bree knew herself to be welcome. Before this night she had doubted that this could be possible. She allowed herself to drink in that blessing as tears pooled in her eyes.

"Thank you, cousine."

Bree watched Rose's face slowly fill with surprise. "For what?" Rose asked.

"For welcoming me. For opening your home to me. But, are you really sure that you want me here? I could just as easily stay at a hotel…" Bree saw Rose start to shake her head, knew she was silently objecting, but Bree persisted. "Cousine, I know all too well what might happen if our uncle finds out."

Rose sighed gustily. "I don't care," she breathed, stepping close enough to wrap her arms around Bree's shoulders.

"And your husband?" Bree asked, concern welling in her voice. "What does he say?"

Rose laughed softly. "Honestly? He quoted his mother. According to him, she would have said, 'Let the Goddess deal with them.' And I am apt to agree." Bree's shoulders shook as Rose stepped back and looked her directly in the eyes. "Bree," Rose affirmed, "you are welcome here. In peace, in shelter and in the Love of the Mother, you are welcome here."

Tears spilled silently down Bree's cheeks. She had yearned for so long to hear those words in this place. Unable to speak and shaking slightly, she pulled Rose to her and hugged her close.

"Thank you," Bree finally managed to whisper. "Thank you."

Releasing her cousine and taking a deep, steadying breath, Bree smiled. "Now, off to bed with you! Your husband will be wondering what we could possibly be chatting about so long."

Rose rolled her eyes. "Oh I don't think so. No doubt he is already snoring like a drunken troll. But, if you insist..." Rose turned, kissed Bree on the cheek and headed out the door. With a parting good night, the door closed leaving Bree alone.

"Let the Goddess deal with them."

Closing her eyes, Bree let the words throb softly around her.

JENNIFER LYNN

CHAPTER SIX

Bree stood a while in the quiet, eyes closed, just breathing deeply. With each exhale, she let it go – the noise of travel... the stray thoughts and emotions lingering from other passengers... the Otherworldly grime of the hospital. Anything other than her own life force, light and soul essence, she released it all back to the Mother, to the great cauldron of Life.

Slowly, a gleam of clarity blossomed to shine in her inner vision, and Bree turned her focus to her own vibration. Her heartbeat called to her. Steady and even, she allowed herself to sink into that rhythm. On and on the pulsation flowed, filling Bree with its constant affirmation of life. *"I am,"* it seemed to whisper. *"I am... I am..."*

Another vibration rippled through Bree's awareness, drawing her attention to her pocket. Opening her eyes to normal awareness, she pulled out her vibrating telephone and frowned at the name and number on the display.

No. Not now, Bree rued silently and put away the telephone.

A pile of floor pillows caught her eye and Bree smiled. *Just like Rose to think of everything...* Pulling two of the pillows out into the middle of the floor, Bree settled herself onto them and closed her eyes.

Continuing to relax into herself, Bree exhaled slowly, allowing the weight of her body to release toward the floor. The hard wood welcomed her, offering its solid comfort, its steady reassurance of support. With each exhale Bree relaxed into that support, her tired body finally releasing the tension of the extended day.

Now well grounded, Bree sent her awareness out to the edges of her being. She shifted her focus onto her inhale and began to drink in loving light. Drawing it in with each breath, she let Love fill her until her energy body shimmered in her inner vision.

Keeping her eyes closed, Bree began to clear the room, sending outward from her body a gentle light that cascaded around her. Flowing in concentric circles, rings of light rippled outward with each exhale, gliding farther and farther, until they reached the very corners of the room. As each new circle washed to the edge and unified into a boundary, the room began to glow, filling Bree's inner vision with radiant, opalescent light.

"Peace be in this space…" Bree knew these words so well. They flowed effortlessly, like the light spilling to fill the room. "Peace be in this land… Peace be in this Walking…"

She paused to breathe deeply. Around her the room softened into quiet, into the Grace of Peace. Allowing her awareness to expand to the directions, she called once more to the *Airds*, to the sacred directions of the Celtic Wheel.

"Great Spirit of North, the home of earth and the wisdom of remembering… Great Spirit of the North I call to you in Peace. Come, join this circle. Shelter and hold this circle in the Grace of Your Love."

A subtle change filled the north of the room, as a pressure like a wall of energy now stood sheltering her. Bree bowed her head in gratitude, then allowed her awareness to flow to the right, sunwise, into the east.

"Great Spirit of East, the home of air and the wisdom of birthing... Great Spirit of East I call to you in Peace. Come, join this circle. Shelter and hold this circle in the Grace of Your Love."

Again that subtle pressure blossomed in the east of the room and Bree could sense the wall of shelter expand around her. Offering silent gratitude, Bree bowed her head and allowed her awareness to flow sunwise to the space behind her, into the south.

"Great Spirit of South, the home of fire and the wisdom of becoming... Great Spirit of South I call to you in Peace. Come, join this circle. Shelter and hold this circle in the Grace of Your Love."

That familiar, rippling pressure expanded and curved to arc around Bree, filling the south of the room. Again Bree bowed her head in silent gratitude before allowing her awareness to flow ever sunward, into the west.

"Great Spirit of West, the home of water and the wisdom of returning... Great Spirit of West I call to you in Peace. Come, join this circle. Shelter and hold this circle in the Grace of Your Love."

Now that pressure expanded to encircle Bree, becoming a solid, circular shield of Love and Grace and Light. Again Bree bowed her head silently offering her gratitude.

"Great Spirit of Center, the home of ether and the wisdom of Sovereignty... Great Spirit of Center I call to you in Peace. Come, join this circle. Shelter and hold this circle in the Grace of Your Love."

The light radiated outward to the circle of energy encompassing Bree, sealing the circle and securing the space for Working. Certain in the clarity of that encompassing, Bree bowed her head in silent gratitude.

"Great Mother, Sacred Three, bless this Working. Guide this Working with the Love, the Wisdom, the Peace of your Grace."

The circle now set, Bree was ready to begin. Letting her being pulsate with Love, Bree filled her awareness with one word.

Emily...

CHAPTER SEVEN

Laughter, joyous and flowing, ripples and cascades to fill Bree's world. The sound kisses her with the wind, lifts her higher, higher.

Her wings pumping, pressing against the air, she flies. Black feathers quiver, dancing in the sunlight. Laughter splashes her, and she rocks upon the wind, her wings shifting to spiral downward, earthward, following the ripple of laughter in the wind.

Her feet touch solid earth, and she is woman again. Her black hair drifts and dances in the sunlight that seems to radiate from everywhere.

Streaks of blue, crimson and gold dance and swirl around her, filling Bree with delight. Laughter peals forth, as Bree closes her eyes, lifts her face skyward and basks in the beauty.

"Hello, Raven Child."

The voice, familiar and commanding, draws a smile to Bree's lips. She opens her eyes to see Raven, her friend and Ally standing before her. Bree knows it is Raven who has carried her into this Walking.

"Hello, Raven."

Laughter ripples around them, and Raven shifts her gaze to follow it.

Bree, too, turns to see a familiar red blaze turning, turning, turning amidst a sea of wildflowers. Hands – strong and supple – glide, palms cupped skyward to drink in the radiance. Peals of sheer delight waft and bathe Bree. She smiles at the sight.

"Yes," Bree whispers thoughtfully, "this is her place of happiness, wild and dancing among the flowers."

Raven chirrups softly beside her, calling Bree gently back to the Walking. Bree nods to Raven and steps toward her aunt.

Recognizing her niece, Emily's eyes widen and she runs to sweep Bree up into a swirling embrace. Through endless laughter, Emily bubbles, "Raven Child! Raven Child!" Then she sobers suddenly and turns to Bree, face to face. "But, what are you doing here?"

"Looking for you," Bree answers softly, allowing love to flow outward and caress her aunt in gentle waves. "Aunt," she begins, "how came you to be dancing in this field?"

Emily looks around her, eyes wide as if in surprise. "I'm... I'm not sure... It was dark... and then... then it wasn't. And I was here."

Bree sighs. "While your soul dances here in the Wild of the Otherworld, in the physical world your body lingers unconscious, untended." Bree watches Emily, sees the light of her soul body flicker, absorbing this information. As Emily turns questioning eyes to her niece, Bree confirms, "Your body lies in a coma, Aunt."

By instinct and training, Emily looks to her feet. There, beneath her stretches a silver chord, one end attached to herself, the other disappearing into the distance. While the end closest to her twines in a plait solid and thick, flowing onward broken strands splay and bend away from the weave. The further she traces the plait, the more ragged and tenuous it appears. With a gasp, she discovers the center of the chord has ruptured completely. Only the outer-most strands still struggle to hold.

"It is fraying." *Emily's whisper reveals her surprise.*

"Yes, Aunt. It is," *Bree confirms.*

"Why?"

Emily's sincere question silences Bree. Surely, surely, she must know. She must understand.

"You are dying," *Bree explains quietly.* "Aunt, it is time. You must make a choice."

JENNIFER LYNN

CHAPTER EIGHT

"She must choose."

Bree sat with Rose at the kitchen table. The journey had left Bree restless and she had wandered into the kitchen out of habit. She heard the soft footsteps of her cousine coming down the hall while setting the kettle on the stove. One look and Bree had known... Rose heard her moving about the kitchen and, anxious for news, joined her. Without a word, Bree had poured an extra cup of tea. She knew anything else was pointless.

Bree offered what she could of the journey. She wanted to tell Rose more, to assure her that Emily was well, happy, even rejoicing in the Otherworld. But it was not her story to tell. For reasons still unknown to Bree, Emily had refused to allow contact with Rose, and Bree needed to honor that choice. Instead, she explained that Emily's silver chord had been damaged, that it was fraying, and that Emily stood now at a crossroads.

Bree watched as Rose listened patiently, stoically, her eyes fixed on her teacup. When Rose said nothing, Bree continued.

"She must choose. Either Emily must reclaim her life and return to her body, or she must let go and make Transition. And only Emily may choose."

Bree waited, but Rose said nothing.

Bree understood. She would be quiet, too, were she in a similar situation. In a way, she was. After all, Emily was her foster mother. Bree searched Rose's blank expression. Behind the calm exterior, Bree sensed sorrow, raw and aching.

"And she understands?" Rose's voice held steady.

Bree nodded. "Your mother understands. She understands the significance of the choice and the need to choose. And she knows how to find me once she is ready."

CHAPTER NINE

After the marathon of flights from Shannon to Newark, to her arrival in Seattle and the night's Working, Bree fell in a heap onto the bed in Rose's guest room. Too tired to undress, she pulled the quilt over her shoulders and closed her eyes. Sinking into oblivion, she slept without dream, without awareness of the room or household around her.

The mournful sound of rain pattering greeted Bree as her eyes opened onto a world of semi-darkness. For a moment, she thought she had slept through the day and into the evening. Then she remembered – she was in Seattle.

The clock on the nightstand told her it was almost noon. That, at least, explained the quiet in the house.

A note on the kitchen table greeted Bree in Rose's clear, looping, cursive script. "Gone to the hospital to be with Emily. I want her to know I support her, no matter what she decides." Bree sensed her cousine's courage etched and aching through the words on the page. She had forgotten the depths of her cousine's strength. The rest of the note left Bree laughing. "Lunch is in the fridge."

From the ecstasy to the laundry, Bree chuckled as she opened the refrigerator door to see what was for lunch.

A bowl of homemade potato and leek soup rested on the second shelf under a single red rose. Bree smiled at the welcoming touch of her cousine. Certain that a loaf of fresh brown bread awaited her in the breadbox, Bree's mouth watered as she pulled the bowl out onto the counter.

The soup heated quickly, once Bree found the cupboard of pots. Of course, the delay offered her an excuse to indulge in a few extra slices of Rose's brown bread, as fortification for her search. Placing the kettle to boil over a low flame, Bree carried her lunch to the table and sat down. She rested her hands on either side of the bowl, palms skyward, closed her eyes and bowed her head.

"Great Mother," Bree began, "blessed is your bounty. Blessed is your Grace. Blessed is your Love. Thank you for the blessings of this food, this life, this day. *Sin é.*"

The steam from the soup drifted across Bree's face and her stomach growled. She had spoken a blessing for the meal, but, as hungry as she was, Bree could not move from her position of prayer.

Something must be missing, she realized. Keeping her eyes closed, she allowed herself to settle into stillness and listened.

A smile spread slowly across her face. "Mother Bríghid," Bree called softly, "thank you for your Love, your shelter and the gifts of family. *Sin é.*"

A sensation of warmth spread through Bree's body, her personal sign of a prayer received. Nodding silently, Bree opened her eyes, picked up her spoon and bowl, and walked over to the sliding glass door behind the table. Stepping out onto the deck, Bree poured three spoonfuls of soup onto the grass below.

BEING HERE

"With gratitude to the Land Spirits, the *Sídhe* Spirits and the Mothers of this land. Thank you for your loving hospitality."

Warmth spreading anew within her, Bree smiled, nodded and returned to the table. Settling into her seat this time, she bent hungrily over the bowl.

The kettle was steaming by the time Bree finished her meal. Leaving her now-clean bowl and spoon in the wooden drying rack, she poured herself a cup of tea and wandered toward the sofa.

As she crossed the den, the image of a woman smiling at her flickered through her awareness. She stopped and looked more closely, using both ordinary and inner sight, but this time saw nothing. She shifted her head side to side slightly, adjusting her position a few times and looking in the direction of the impression.

There... She was not dreaming. On a shelf, half-hidden behind other family photos, the face of her mother, Bríde, smiled at her.

Bree set her cup of tea down on the end table, walked over to the bookcase and let her eyes dance over the collection of photos. Faces greeted her from across the generations... some smiling, some laughing, others with expressions firm as stone. Bree recognized or remembered the events captured in many of the photos. She even kept some of them on a similar shelf in her own cottage in Ireland. The collection acted as an altar to her ancestors, a way of honoring the members of her lineage, the living and the ones who came before. Bree lifted the photo of her mother, Emily, and their mother, Brígh, off the shelf and smiled.

"Hello, Mother."

"Beannachtaí, a stór..." Her mother's voice whispered blessings from the Otherworld.

"You know I am here, in Seattle, don't you?" Bree spoke to her mother, connecting through the photo.

"Of course," came her reply.

Naturally. Bree nodded, remembering.

Her mother had always been there for her, from the nighttime stories of her childhood to her first journey steps in the Otherworld. Following Emily's advice, Bree had sought her mother's assistance from across the Veil in the early days of her shamanic training.

"The universe pulsates..." Bríde had explained, "... with the world of physical life and the world of soul. They are two halves of one whole, interconnected and flowing one into the other. Both halves need each other, inter-penetrate each other and are incomplete without the other, and what happens in one informs and often determines what may happen in the other."

"Most people live aware of only one side of the Veil at a time," her mother's voice flowed again through Bree's awareness. "But as a *Bean feasa*, you have the ability to live in *both* worlds, simultaneously. One of the *Aes Dána*, the Gifted, you can walk in This World, the Otherworld and the spaces in between."

Bree placed the photo of her mother on the coffee table in front of her and sat back, settling into the sofa. Gazing into the picture of her mother's smiling face, Bree realized this was no ordinary moment of simple remembering. This was a sending, an intentional gifting of memory from her mother.

Why, Bree wondered. What message could her mother be sending through this memory? Bree did not know. For now, all she could do was let it flow and trust the answer would come.

She closed her eyes, exhaled and let the vision carry her.

"Why, mother?" The voice of a much younger Bree echoed in her mind as the memory resumed, drawing her deeper into vision. "Why would the universe need someone so gifted?"

"Every flame must be tended," Bríde had replied, the scene around her morphing into a single flame burning in an ancient, earthen brazier.

Gazing into that flame, the world had opened before Bree. The faces of loved ones and strangers alike had rippled into and out of view. She witnessed the earth in its becoming, even the cosmos spiraling in its endless dance. As her mind gaped in awe, a voice – feminine, ancient, loving – filled her awareness.

"The flame is creation unfolding. In it Dark and Light dance with Mystery."

"To tend the Sacred Flame of Life is to cultivate balance, flow and Oneness," Bríde had continued, supporting the awakening within Bree. "And to tend the Sacred Flame, you must be able to see it in *all* of its manifestations, This Worldly and Otherworldly."

A shift in the dance of shadow, light and Mystery had drawn Bree's attention. She had watched as a woman, ancient yet youthful, stepped out of the flame and walked toward Bree and her mother. Fiery radiance shimmered beneath the plain, white linen scarf draped over the woman's head. Her eyes glittered like starlight and, held in that gaze, Bree sensed herself washed in light to the depths of her soul.

"Mother," Bríde whispered, bowing her head as the woman came to stand before her.

"Beannachtaí, mo leanbh... Blessings, my child."

Bree heard the unspoken words of blessing as the woman stepped forward and kissed her mother's forehead. Fiery light poured through her mother, radiating downward to fill the depths of her energy body. When her mother rose and opened her eyes, light streamed from them.

"As the first-born daughter, you are a guardian of the Sacred Flame." Bríde's voice sounded softer, fuller, deeper somehow.

Bree knew the change was important. Her mind urged her to consider the shift, but she could not. Utterly captivated, Bree could not stop staring at the woman standing beside her mother and in front of herself. She looked so... familiar.

Who is she? Bree ached to know.

With a simple gesture of the hand, her mother answered her unspoken question. "Bríghid can show you the way."

Bree vibrated, mind body and soul. Eddies of energy rippled and pulsated through every aspect of her, setting her entire being to trembling. The sensation puzzled her. She felt no fear... quite the opposite. She stood, bathed in a love so pure, so compassionate, so *complete,* her soul had simply welcomed it.

She had found herself bowing, instinctively honoring... "Mother Bríghid."

The goddess smiled, releasing rays of light to stream around Bree. *"Beannachtaí, mo Ghrá... Blessings, my Love."*

Reaching to take Bríghid's outstretched hands, Bree stepped into the flame. Power flowed around and through her, bathing her from the inside out, stripping away layer upon layer of perceptions, images of herself crafted out of the experiences of her life. Awe filled Bree as she watched the self she had known falling away, burnt to nothing, like garments in a fire. She felt no pain, knew only tenderness.

Through each fiery caress, Bríghid's voice held her. *"Love is the fundamental vibration. Everything is sacred, born of the Lovemaking of the Mother, Father and Creator, of the sacred fire of life. As my first-born daughter, you are a guardian of that Sacred Flame. You are the tender, the tending, and the tended."*

Bree had been emptied. The fire had burnt it all away. Everything she believed herself to be was gone. For a moment, she wondered if she would disappear entirely. But Bríghid squeezed her hands tenderly, shifting the dance of the flame within Bree. She began to drink in the fire, drawing the light in, and filling her energy body with the power of the flame.

Bríghid's voice continued to steady her. *"All beings are sacred and have a place on the circle. Each teaches a unique wisdom, a way of walking with the Sacred. As a Bean feasa, you will work with many Allies to awaken your inner wisdom and to learn to live as Love in every way. You will begin with the five animals of the Celtic Wheel."*

Bree's hands fell to her sides as Bríghid shifted to stand behind her. Gently pressing her hand to the back of Bree's heart, the goddess began the introductions.

"Bear teaches you to walk in harmony with the Earth, at peace with the Great Mother."

In silent wonder, Bree shivered as the light of the Sacred Flame trembled into a blaze. She watched as, emerging out of that flare, Bear walked on all fours toward her and Mother Bríghid. Bear moved slowly, purposefully, with tenderness and grace, her eyes firmly upon Bree. Coming to stand before her, Bear rose onto her hind legs and placed her front paws upon Bree's chest.

Bree's energy field thrummed with the strong yet tender pressure of Bear's paws. Light, energy, life force – Bree had been unsure which, if not all – poured into her through the contact, etching onto her chest the outline of Bear's touch. Drawn into Bear's gaze, Bree bent closer and closer, until her nose had touched the soft leather of Bear's snout. They stood there, breathing nose to nose, gently sharing their essence, until – on Bree's inhale – Bear stepped fully into her, becoming one with her.

Power flooded through Bree, rippling in all directions as Bear settled into her. With a gasp, she realized the light around her, the light of the Sacred Flame had begun to tremble again. This time she sensed more than heard Bríghid's words.

"Eagle opens the gift of vision, shows you how to scry the unknown and choose."

Fiery brilliance flashed around Bree, dancing in streaks that roiled and coalesced into the shape of Eagle, wings outstretched and pumping slowly. Gliding on hidden thermals, Eagle coasted toward Bree, banked into a close spiral around her. Bree sensed Eagle scrying her, gazing into the very depths of her being, reading her soul. She wondered what he might see there. Then his eyes locked with hers and, her vision blurring, he flew straight into her, merging his essence with her own. Bree felt her arms taking on the soft down of feathers, stretching wide in flight. But she had never moved.

Blinking her vision back to clear, Bree sensed the now-familiar shift in the Sacred Flame as Bríghid's voice called her onward.

"Stag awakens within you the thrumming power of the Wild, teaches you to hear the heartbeat of the Mother and to live in harmony with the unfolding of Life."

The Flame blazed anew around her – no, *through* her, she realized – and Bree sensed the pounding of hooves upon her energy body, even before Stag emerged from the fire. Leaping into form and landing directly before her, Stag stood tall and strong, front hooves dancing a heartbeat upon the earth. Bree's soul pounded with that heartbeat, welcoming the embrace of its rhythm without question. As each beat drew her more deeply into its pulsation, Stag stepped closer and closer until, eyes locked, he stepped into her.

Power – raw, wild, *natural* – flooded through Bree, as the heartbeat pulsed, filling her awareness. She needed to move, to honor the rhythm coursing through her, to turn her head and listen to the Wild. Drawing her right ear closer to the ground, she struggled briefly to steady herself under the weight of antlers… *his* antlers, growing out of *her* head! Raising herself upright and standing with a new sense of balance, Bree and Stag had become one.

Still Bríghid called her onward, as the Sacred Flame prepared to blaze once more.

"Salmon guides you through the flow, unveils the wisdom of the emotions and the journey home."

Fiery light rippled in blazing arcs, flowing and undulating all around Bree, as a sense of being watched washed through her. Looking more closely, eyes seemed to stare back at her from within the copper-red fire. Even the undulating looked more like scales on a tail. Following the blaze as it flowed to pool before her, Bree smiled as Salmon emerged, head first, out of the fiery waters. His eyes – ancient and deep as the sea – called to Bree, and she bent forward. With a flash of light, Salmon leapt into her.

The sound of waters rushing filled Bree's awareness, as the fire continued to undulate and flow around her. The current pressed against her, pervasive and insistent, but Bree simply paused. Gazing through the eyes of Salmon, Bree sensed the journey streaming in all directions... downstream, upstream, and here and now. Hovering in the flow, skin yielding to scales and gills opening along her neck, Bree learned to breathe as Salmon.

Bree shivered, as the rhythm of the Sacred Flame started to shift yet again. This time she sensed the change within herself, emerging from deep inside her own energies. Wondering at the new experience, she heard Bríghid calling.

"Raven integrates and strips away the old to birth the new."

Again, fiery light blazed. Everywhere Bree looked – around her, through her, *within* her – the Sacred Flame shone back to her. Within that radiance, Bree sensed a presence moving, a shadow inside the light. Closing her eyes and gazing into the darkness, wings stretched into view. A presence pressed into her, called to her from inside the darkness. Shifting her focus to track the call, Bree gasped as Raven flew into her, filling her instantly from toes to head.

Rich, fertile darkness flowed to the very depths of her, stretched into feathers the shades of midnight that spread to the edges of her. Silent with wonder, Bree traced the rippling waves of purple, blue and black now covering her, flowing with the curve of Raven's head. With a flash of blinding light, Raven's eye blinked into view and seared itself upon Bree, completing the merging.

Bear, Eagle, Stag, Salmon and Raven... Bree knew they had gifted her that day in the Sacred Flame, with Bríghid's blessing. Here, on Rose's couch, she knew those gifts were with her still. She could sense their presence even now, so many years later. She continued to work with them, to learn from them, and needed only to shift her focus briefly to perceive their power coursing through her. These Allies had become closer than friends. They were her family.

Bree gasped softly, her mother's message becoming clear. That day in the flame, Bríghid had spoken true... *"These five Allies and I are ever with you."*

Bree still remembered the touch of that flame, the fierce coolness of the fire that cleanses and empowers but never burns. On the sofa, Bree's energy field pulsated, replenished with the memory. Her chest filled with warmth as she sensed Bríghid's hand over her heart.

"Remember," Bríghid's voice – feminine, ancient, loving – flowed through her. *"You are my Love. You are my Love. You are my Love."*

The soft, crispness of white linen draped around Bree's shoulders as Bríghid enfolded her in a mantle of loving shelter. Exhaling deeply, Bree allowed herself to sink into and drift with that Love.

Floating past the edge of awareness toward sleep, Bree heard Bríghid's voice echo softly once more.

"I am with you – always and all ways."

CHAPTER TEN

Bree's telephone rang, jostling her awake. Blinking herself back to full consciousness, she scanned the room for the disturbance that had pulled her from sleep. Finding nothing obvious, Bree settled back onto the sofa.

I must have been dreaming, she mused.

Her telephone rang again and Bree jumped slightly. Pulling it out of her pocket, Bree saw Rose's number staring back at her on the display. Still drifting groggily, she answered it.

"You're up!" Rose's voice greeted Bree.

"Well, I'm awake now," Bree mumbled, stretching like a cat on the sofa. "But I wouldn't exactly claim to be up."

"Mmmm." Her cousine must be driving. The connection had the hollow, distant sound of a hands-free, speaker phone. "And does awake constitute rested and ready for amusement?"

Bree realized only too late the correct answer was no. Instead she replied through a yawn, "I suppose. What's up?"

"Dinner..." Rose paused before adding, "...with family."

Too late, Bree snapped to attention. "With family?" She didn't need to be more precise with her question. Rose would know *exactly* what Bree meant.

"Heather has decided to play hostess. I told her that you are in town and had been to see Mom. She got so excited she invited the family to dinner, at her place. And yes, *himself* is expected to attend."

Trapped! Bree's body tensed. Her heart pounded as if she had been backed into a corner. She could say no, but that would be no small insult to Rose and their cousine Heather. And Bree liked Heather.

Bree still thought of Heather as a little girl in hand-stitched clothes and pigtails. She and her younger brother, Connor, had home-schooled with Emily and had often been underfoot. Bree could still see them covered in mud, chasing ghosts around the yard, and playing hide-and-seek in the chicken coop. Second cousines and separated by five years, Bree remembered being friendly with Heather, but never as sister-like as with Rose. She wondered what kind of woman Heather had grown up to be.

"Bree?" Rose's voice called through the silence. "Bree? Did I lose you?"

If only, Bree thought, then realized that a dropped call would give her time to craft an escape. She waited a moment longer, hoping the call would spontaneously disconnect as a sign that she could, indeed, say no without regret. But the connection remained strong.

"I'm here." Bree sighed. "What time should I be ready?"

CHAPTER ELEVEN

Rain, cold and grey, streaked the window of Rose's guest room. "The Tears of the Goddess…" Bree whispered into the relentless pattering.

The rhythm of the falling rain pounded through her awareness, then blurred into an unexpected syncopation. Tones stretched and blended, harmonizing into a human voice. Singing through the rain, Bree heard Emily's voice, calling from a past Bree thought she had forgotten.

"The waters that feed our earth, that fall from our skies, that flow in our rivers and that slake our bodies, these waters are the gift of the Great Mother. The waters are the tears of the Goddess, and She sheds those tears that we might live. Everything – every tree, every forest, every animal, including humankind – drinks the tears of the Goddess."

Bree remembered how her younger self had nodded then, her eyes wide in wonder as a woman, full-bodied and heavy-breasted, danced in young Bree's inner vision. The woman had swayed to a sound unimaginable, as tears cascaded from closed eyes to fall upon the earth.

So much sorrow, Bree often wondered. *Why was the Goddess so sad?*

A knock on the door drew Bree's awareness back to the bedroom. Rose called from the other side of the door. "Are you almost ready?"

Bree hesitated, uncertain just how to answer. The honest answer was no, or could she ever be? But, that would be rather rude and unfair to Rose. After all, her cousine had made every effort to put Bree at ease. This was not her doing. Family was family. Hiding would not change that.

Not that I haven't tried, Bree scowled.

She had, in essence, run away, packed her few belongings and fled Seattle, leaving behind everything she loved most in the world. To friends and family, she left ostensibly for college and stayed away for medical school. In truth, she had fled out of fear... fear of herself, of what she was becoming, and of her family and what might happen should she stay. She had known only one thing for certain – she couldn't figure out who or what she might be under the ever-present criticism of family.

Bree frowned. *Extended family*, she corrected herself.

With her mother on the Otherside, Emily and Rose had become her family on this side of the Veil. They had welcomed Bree and were like her, devoted to the Mystery. As for her father, he loved Bree well enough, even if he never asked any questions.

Another knock rapped quick and insistent. Rose's concern bristled palpably through the door. "Bree?"

"I'm all right," Bree called to her cousine. "Just give me a minute."

Not that another minute would really change anything, Bree rued silently. Sitting in safety on the bed in Rose's guest room, Bree sighed. She could find no peaceful way around it.

"When you cannot go around," the voice of her Salmon Ally echoed patiently in her mind, *"you must go through."*

For a moment, Bree could see them. Bear, Eagle, Stag, Salmon and Raven shimmered with Otherworldly light, flowing around her, enfolding her in a sphere of radiant, blue flame. Silvery light blazed within Bree, sealing the connection with her Allies and the sheltering protection of the circle.

"Very well, Salmon," Bree replied. "Hold me in your Love, shelter me in your Peace, and guide me with your Wisdom." Then she stood up and walked out the bedroom door.

JENNIFER LYNN

CHAPTER TWELVE

"Bree!"

A flash of smile was all Bree saw of her cousine before Heather wrapped her arms around Bree's shoulders and pulled her out of the rain and through the front door. Stumbling into the foyer and surrendering her favorite black fleece to Heather's pulling hands, the living room blurred into Bree's view.

A group of six men hovered near the fireplace, sipping drinks and chatting. Second and third cousines crowded Heather's couch, while a young girl perched casually on the arm.

Bree gaped mentally. *Could that be Ailene's daughter?*

As if in reply to the unspoken question, the woman closest to the girl turned and nodded in silent greeting as Bree was dragged into the hallway.

Definitely Ailene, she noted.

Bree turned sideways and stepped around a woman with beautiful, silver hair hanging in a thick plait down the center of her back. The woman nodded to Bree as she passed. Sparkling, blue eyes held her gaze, and Bree wondered who the silver-haired woman might be. Then Heather tugged onward, and

Bree had to focus as she dodged the extended family milling in the hall.

She had forgotten what these gatherings could be like, the noise of so many confined to spaces slightly too small for them. Were she not a guest of honor, she would have sought refuge outside.

Escorting her into the room and around the circle of faces both familiar and new, Heather kept an arm locked fiercely around Bree's shoulders. Bree did not really mind. Actually, she found it to be rather comforting and so unlike her cousine, at least as Bree remembered her.

"Heather," a man's voice chuckled from behind Bree. "Our cousine is a woman grown. Surely she can stand without your support."

Bree turned to discover a rather tall, lean yet graceful man smiling back at her. His eyes were as full of laughter as they had been as a young man. His hair still blazed brilliantly with that shade of red that proclaimed him Emily's son. As he stepped forward to draw Bree into a welcoming embrace, Bree smiled deeply.

"Declan." Bree whispered tenderly into the privacy of their embrace. In response, Declan gently tightened his hold.

Bree's breath deepened and time seemed to slow, their embrace stretching back to the day Bree had left Seattle. Declan had held her then, too, had whispered tenderly in her ear, "We'll be here, Raven Child." Then he had let her go.

Of her Seattle family, Declan understood Bree the best. They were, she knew, very much alike. Quiet, contemplative and perfectly comfortable with their own company, Declan and Bree had spent most of their time as children alone and outside. At first she had thought him distant and uninterested. He was, after all, five years older. But as she grew, she began to recognize within Declan that same stillness, that same deep, peace-seeking quiet, that she had discovered within herself. *Anam cara*, the Irish would say. Soul friends.

"Welcome back, Raven Child." Declan's voice drew Bree back to the present, back to her cousine's living room and the ever-present gloom of the rain. For the first time since her arrival, she was truly glad to be here.

"Yes, welcome back, Bree."

Bree turned to find her surprised expression reflected in dancing, hazel-green eyes. Eyes, Bree noted, that were now level with her own.

"Connor... you've grown."

Chuckling softly, Connor nodded, strawberry blond hair cascading in curling waves around his smile. "That's what you always say."

It was a game they had played. Connor, the youngest of Emily's home-school brood, had always wanted to be older, to grow up and "be big" like Declan, Bree and Rose. So Bree had encouraged him.

Bree let her eyes dance, tracing the length of Connor from his feet to the top of his head. Then she brought her gaze level, meeting his.

"This time, cousin, it really is true."

Connor could only smile. Stepping forward to embrace his cousine briefly, he nodded. "I suppose it is."

Reunited with her Seattle family and standing now between Declan and Connor, Bree seemed more or less at ease. Even the crucifix on the wall wasn't bothering her tonight.

For so many years she had struggled with that image, wondering how people could embrace an image of terror, torture and death as their sacred icon. *"Everything is sacred,"* her Otherworldly teacher had answered her once. *"Everything – the pain of dissolution and death, the joy of birth and life, and the peace of the places in between – everything has a place in the circle. No one is more sacred than another."*

The telephone in Bree's pocket vibrated, and she stared briefly at the name on the display. With a quiet sigh, Bree put it back in her pocket, unanswered.

Connor chuckled, his eyes dancing with mischief over his glass. "Is that Gwen? Good to know she still keeps tabs on you. Who knows what kind of mischief you might get yourself into otherwise."

Declan shook his head, feigning disgust. "My apologies, Bree. We really do try to teach him manners." He shot his cousin a look of reproach, but Connor saw the merriment in Declan's eyes and laughed heartily.

Inwardly, Bree frowned. At least she could avoid the question, for now. But they would ask again, she reminded herself, searching for a topic to lead them away from the matter of Gwen.

"Uncle!" Heather's voice rang out from the front door.

Bree took a deep, steadying breath. She desperately wanted to run, to cast a *Fáth Fíth*, a cloak of invisibility, upon herself and disappear into the rain. For a moment she considered doing just that. Instead, Bree reminded herself she was an adult. Here, now, she had the undeniable right to choose for herself.

Then Declan and Connor stepped closer to her, sheltering her between them like an honor guard. Breathing deeply of that love, she called again for wisdom.

"When you cannot go around," the voice of Salmon echoed patiently in her mind, *"you must go through."*

JENNIFER LYNN

CHAPTER THIRTEEN

Bree's body tensed. Despite the sheltering company of Declan and Connor, she stood ready for a fight, even expecting one. *Like begets like*, she chided herself and willed her body to relax.

It refused.

Trying a different approach, she turned her focus to the earth and listened for the heartbeat of the Mother.

But her eyes refused to close.

Bree watched in silent dread as two hands reached out from the foyer and passed a wet raincoat into Heather's welcoming arms. She knew Heather was speaking, but she could not follow the words. Her focus was completely occupied with the man now walking into the living room.

He looks well enough, Bree thought as the man who had made her life a living hell stopped to exchange greetings with one of the cousins milling in the hallway. *Maybe he has changed?* Bree wondered silently. *Maybe this time he will act differently?*

Her body tensed, as if to say, *Not very likely*.

Her uncle released the handshake that had held his attention and, chuckling softly, continued walking into the living room. After a cursory nod of greeting to Declan, his eyes locked with Bree's. She stood perfectly still, body tensed and ready, as she watched the smile drain from his face.

"You."

The word poured over Bree, cold as ice water. She shivered slightly, determined to be peaceful. "Hello, Uncle."

Her uncle all but lunged at Bree. "You *will not* speak to me," he hissed between gritted teeth. "Get out! This is no place for the likes of *you*."

His wet raincoat still draped on her arm, Heather stepped into the exchange. Bree watched, body tensed and ready to defend herself, as Heather tried to gentle their uncle, her voice pitched to ease a cranky child.

"Come Uncle, Bree is my guest. This is an evening for family, a blessing for my home."

"A *blessing*?!" Her uncle shouted. "You *dare* welcome a sinner into your home? This, this... *woman* who flouts God's law, who honors false idols and takes to her bed women! You embrace this, this... *heathen*? What bastardized *blessing* can *she* be? Even God would cast her out!"

He glared at Heather, his nose pressed almost to hers. "God killed her mother, cleansed the earth of that tainted blood. Mark my words..." His eyes locked on Bree's. "Her turn will come."

A wave of unspoken shock slammed into Bree. Gasping and reaching for power from the earth to steady herself, a thought flooded in, echoing from all around the room.

"He has gone too far."

The stunned silence shattered into shouting. Voices ricocheted around Bree as heads whirled and turned.

Horrified, Bree struggled to find balance amid the backlash. The past kaleidoscoped in on her, pulling her down in a relentless tide. Images spilled and overlapped... her uncle's face, eyes closed in prayer hovering a breath's edge from her own, his hands painfully pressing a cross into her forehead as water dripped down her face... Bree and Amber, her first girlfriend, pressed back to back, tensed to fight the men slowly surrounding them... hands forcing Bree's mouth open as her uncle poured something cold and sour down her throat...

No! She screamed mentally. *No, that is over. You are an adult now.*

Another wave crashed into Bree. This one burned with outrage and threatened to drown her.

Still fighting the torrent of overlapping memories, Bree watched the eruption unfold in painful, slow motion... Declan and Connor stepping forward, shouting while attempting to shield Bree bodily... Rose forcibly parting bodies across the room in a desperate attempt to come to Bree's side... and Heather, poor Heather, her beautiful smile wrenched into horror, then shock and despair.

At the middle of it all, Bree stood shaking. Her teenage self urged Bree to run. *Not again. Never again!* Her adult self assured teenaged Bree all would be well. *Just breathe. We are safe*. Churned between the past and the present, Bree silently wished herself elsewhere.

"Look, Raven Child..." the familiar voice of Salmon rose over the chaos, filling Bree's ears and mind. *"Look with your inner vision and see the source of their outrage."*

The memories flooded relentlessly, overlapping with the family energies ricocheting around the room. Attempting to steady herself in the sudden onslaught was about all Bree could manage. Focusing on the present, on the situation at hand, offered solid ground.

Now her Ally was asking her to scry deeper into the chaos, to let herself shift *into* the eruption. The instruction seemed counter-intuitive. But Bree knew Salmon well, trusted Salmon. She knew his instruction held purpose. Leaning into that trust, she took a deep breath, closed her eyes and shifted her awareness...

... Energy sizzles and howls, like winds whipping the frenzy before a storm. Aching, throbbing in the growing anger, Bree can sense the lightning swelling, preparing to strike. It builds all around her, encompasses her, presses upon her. Instinctively she reaches inside for loving light, prepares to create a shield to protect herself, a personal lightning rod to siphon off the assault.

"No, Raven Child," Salmon's voice ripples with the roiling energies. "No. See the Truth behind the appearance. Remember... energy must flow. From the point of activation to the point of manifestation, energy must flow. Look. Look into the true heart of the flow. See the Truth of the unfolding."

Silently placing her trust in Salmon, Bree shifts her focus and releases a ray of light to track the raging eddies.

"From activation to manifestation," she whispers, guiding the ray of light. She gasps as the light dances from the faces of her family to land upon her uncle. Again, Bree releases a ray of light dancing across the eddies. It, too, lands firmly upon her uncle.

"Three reveals the Mystery," Bree whispers as she releases a third and final ray of light. Truth illumines Bree as the ray of light stops on her uncle.

"It's him. They are angry with him," Bree exhales her surprise.

"Yes, Raven Child."

Her family supported her. Bree had never realized.

She thought they were glad to be rid of her. A child, dumped upon them by a father too overwhelmed, lost to sorrow and unable to care after his wife's death, Bree had always known herself to be the outcast.

Emily had tried. She had welcomed Bree into her home, but Bree had always been different. In the end, those differences had sparked anger, conflict and division. When she left Seattle, she thought her family had exhaled with relief. But here, in her cousine's living room, proof to the contrary danced before her.

Salmon's voice echoed in her mind. *"Yes, Raven Child."*

That sense of belonging steadied Bree. Letting herself breathe it in, she stood, eyes closed in the center of the storm.

I belong, she inhaled deeply. A flicker of light pulsed, dimming the flood of memories still raging in Bree's awareness. *I belong*, she inhaled again, drawing the light from a flicker to a ray. *I belong*, she inhaled a third time, the ray broadening into a beam.

Light now poured into Bree's energy body. With each breath, that light pulsated, rippled and shimmered, imbuing her with opalescent radiance. Bathed in that light, the flood of memories dissolved and a sense of ease began to fill Bree. As ease blossomed into peace, she opened her eyes.

Chaos raged on around Bree. Declan and Connor remained in front of her, screaming her defense. Rose had joined them. Breathing deeply into healing peace, Bree stepped around them, tried to quiet them. But they were lost to the storm.

Bree smelled ozone charging. How? How could she break the pattern, dispel the chaos and invite healing?

"The wall... Look to the wall." Her Raven Ally called, guiding Bree.

"You're joking," Bree replied in her mind.

"Through death comes rebirth..." Raven chirruped.

With a steadying breath and a call for healing Grace, Bree lifted the crucifix off the wall.

The room fell silent. Bree's skin prickled as eyes throughout the room turned to watch her.

Bree walked toward her uncle, crucifix in hand. He stammered silently, unable to voice whatever emotion slowly etched him in red.

As her Raven Ally perched on her shoulder, Bree raised the crucifix in her hands, drawing it to rest upon her chest. "Tell me, Uncle," she spoke softly, gently, letting loving light flow outward from her being. "If God truly despised me as you claim, would He allow me to hold His cherished icon and stand untouched?"

No one moved.

Her uncle's face contorted slowly into a sneer. He stood, expectant, even triumphant. But nothing happened.

Shifting her hold, Bree enfolded the crucifix in a hug. From the Otherworld, Raven pressed Bree's head downward toward her chest. Bowing with Raven's wisdom, Bree offered the crucifix a kiss.

Her uncle scowled. "How dare you!" He growled and ripped the crucifix from Bree's arms. "How *dare* you profane this sacred icon!" Clutching the crucifix to his chest, he turned toward the others standing around the room. "Now, *now* you see! Remove this *heathen* at once!"

Still, no one moved.

Raven chirruped and edged her way along Bree's shoulder to whisper in her ear. With each Otherworldly word, a deep sense of Grace flowed through Bree. Light poured through her, connecting her to the earth below and the sky above. Standing in that flow, Bree knew she truly belonged.

Centered and at peace, Bree broke the silence with Raven's wisdom. "Strange, Uncle. I recall the Bible teaching that Christ proffered acts of love and compassion."

Then, with Declan and Conner trailing proudly behind her, Bree walked into the kitchen.

CHAPTER FOURTEEN

"Well, I've never been called a heathen before."

Bree brooded quietly from her seat at Rose's kitchen table. Her grief thickened as she watched snap-shot images from the evening at Heather's – and another clash with her uncle – swirl in her inner vision and the Caol Ina single malt in her glass.

"You're joking!" Rose laughed in reply.

Bree shook her head sadly, searching back through memories. "Nope." She paused, then added thoughtfully, "At least, not in *this* lifetime."

From across the table Bree watched Rose's jaw drop slightly as she stared. Silenced and serious for the moment, Rose's eyes scanned Bree's face, as if searching for something hidden. Then, with a snort, her cousine fell to laughing again.

Rose, Bree realized, had been laughing since their return to the sanctuary of her kitchen. *Maybe she is right...* Bree wondered. Allowing herself to be carried in the flow, this time Bree chuckled with her. Reviewing the turmoil of the evening's events, laughter really seemed to be the best option.

"I can't believe you threw him out of Heather's house!" Bree shook her head, chuckling harder and harder until she gave in to laughter. As tears pooled at the corner of her eyes, a knot deep inside her belly released. She had to admit — it was good to laugh. It was better still to be in Rose's kitchen.

"Yup," Rose was toasting herself, her glass of whiskey raised high in the air. "It felt blessedly delightful, too! Didn't even allow him to put his coat on!"

Bree beamed at her cousine. "To heathens!" Bree called, offering her glass for the toast.

"To heathens!" Rose managed to clink and empty her glass before she lost herself again in laughter.

So natural. Nothing could be more natural, Bree marveled, than to be here, sitting in Rose's kitchen, laughing. For a moment Bree wondered why she had ever left.

Rose cleared her throat and faced Bree. Leaning an elbow upon the table, her cousine attempted to look serious. As Bree watched Rose's features contort from a grin to a puckered scowl to a lopsided grimace, she stifled a chuckle.

"Oh, Bree, I've been meaning to ask. How is Gwen? Did you leave her in Ireland? Or did she fly back to Saint Louis when you left?"

Bree gasped quietly, bending forward and covering her shock with a cough. She had not expected that question, not in the aftermath of the evening nor in the joyful peace of Rose's kitchen. Shifting her eyes protectively to her glass, she willed her suddenly taut body to relax.

No, Bree breathed, *not now. Not yet.*

Finishing the contents of her glass in a single gulp, Bree stood up from the table. Before Rose could utter another word, Bree turned, muttered "Good night" and pulled the door of the guest room closed behind her.

The darkness of the bedroom engulfed Bree. She stood, heart aching, longing to disappear. A gentle lapping washed over her as Rose approached and knocked softly on the door. Tears sliding down her cheeks, Bree closed her eyes.

She didn't dare move much less speak. She knew – one word would bring it all here.

Into the silence, Bree heard Rose whisper "Good night" before the soft patter of her footsteps disappeared down the hall.

Bree's shoulders sagged with exhaustion and grief. Opening her eyes, she discovered she was not alone. There, but not entirely, the ghostly image of a woman sighed and stepped forward to draw Bree into her arms.

Tears welling slowly in her eyes, Bree shuddered and let herself cry.

JENNIFER LYNN

CHAPTER FIFTEEN

The smell of bacon woke her. Bree rolled over and inhaled deeply. Make that bacon *and* fresh coffee.

"Nectar of the gods," she mumbled, pulling herself out of bed and into yesterday's jeans and her favorite dragon tee shirt. Dressed well enough for Saturday breakfast, she opened the door to the guest room and followed the aroma like a homing signal to the kitchen.

A mug of steaming, black coffee welcomed Bree to the table. Sliding into her seat with the first mouthful, she closed her eyes and sighed.

"Too strong?" Rose turned to smile at her cousine, lifting her gaze briefly from her griddle.

Opening her eyes, Bree returned the smile. "Never."

"Aunt Bree!"

A flash of light danced into the kitchen and stopped just short of Bree's seat at the table. To Bree's inner vision, the light seemed to flow on toward her, reaching out as if to embrace her before lurching back into the willowy form of the young girl now standing in front of her.

Suddenly shy with remembered manners, the girl dropped her chin and pulled her hands behind her back.

"You probably don't remember me," the girl whispered.

"Let me see..." Bree began playfully. Reluctantly placing her coffee mug on the table, she leaned forward as if to inspect the young girl.

As if I wouldn't know Rose's daughter anywhere. The girl's energetic pattern was so similar to her mother's. But the flaming hair and that nose screamed the proof.

"Hmmm... fiery red hair... long, willowy limbs... hazel eyes... yes, yes... You must be Fiona!"

Being remembered by the aunt who had named her – despite having seen her only twice since – was too much for the girl. Her face flowing into brilliance with a radiant smile, Fiona lunged laughing into her aunt's arms. Bree shifted her coffee mug to safety and returned the embrace.

Rose emerged from behind her griddle, laughing. Placing a plate of freshly cooked bacon on the table beside Bree's coffee mug, Rose chided her daughter. "Come, Fiona. Let your aunt finish her first cup of coffee."

The girl's face fell. "Do I have to leave?"

Bree shook her head briefly, but remained quiet, not sure what else Rose may have had in mind to accompany the coffee and bacon.

"No, just let your aunt wake up a bit." Rose chuckled.

Delighted to be in the kitchen with the women, Fiona began turning circles, loosing her flaming red hair to spiral and dance. The flashes of red caught and held Bree's awareness. Suddenly, it was all Bree could see… wave upon wave upon wave of flaming red, flowing, spiraling in an endless dance.

Still turning circles, Fiona began to sing. "Aunt Breeeee! Aunt Breeeee! Aunt Breeeee!"

Or was it Fiona singing? Slipping slowly into trance, Bree thought she could hear another voice singing, calling her by name.

Yes. Someone *was* calling her, calling from across the Veil.

With a breath, her training engaged. Letting her eyes sink closed, Bree exhaled and followed the sound of her name…

"…*Bree!*"

Light – crimson-gold and incandescent – dapples and dances before Bree's eyes. Cascading in streaming prisms, the light ripples, echoing the sound of her name.

"*Bree!*"

Sinking into the flow, Bree lets the dance carry her.

"*Bree!*"

Her awareness follows the light, swirling, spinning circles that shimmer and pulsate.

"*Bree!*"

A sea of light carries her, rocks her gently, bathes her in crimson and gold.

"Bree!"

She rocks gently, carried upon incandescent waters in a dugout. Across the waters, from the shore a woman stands waving.

"Emily..." Bree breathes the name as a whisper.

The woman nods, smiles and lifts her arms in beckoning.

The dugout turns, rocks gently toward the shore as golden light blazes across the waters.

"It seems breakfast will have to wait."

Rose lifted questioning eyes to Bree.

She shrugged. "Seems I have a message to attend to."

Rose nodded, her hazel eyes clear with understanding. "Do you want a Second?"

Bree sensed her cousine's need to be useful. It chafed against her awareness, like sandpaper rubbing her skin. She sympathized, of course. Rose was accustomed to helping. But now, as her mother hovered between life and death, her cousine was effectively shut out. Frustrated, all Rose could do was wait.

Both Bree and Rose understood and honored the sacred cycles of Birth, Life and Death. Initiates of the Mystery, both women celebrated death as another form of birth, as an opening into a different form of existence. Death held no loss, only a beginning.

Bree could still hear Emily's voice, guiding the girls through their lessons... *"We all come into this world owing a death..."*

But... Emily was Rose's mother. Of course Rose would want to help.

"No, cousine, not yet," Bree replied, rising and heading for the guest room. "But, perhaps you and Fiona should eat without me."

Turning to close the guest room door, Bree saw Rose watching quietly.

JENNIFER LYNN

CHAPTER SIXTEEN

Bathed in crimson-gold light, Bree rocks gently, carried in a dugout upon incandescent waters. A shoreline nears and the boat shudders to a halt. Bree steps out, her feet sinking slightly into warm sand.

"Blessed is the Mother," *Bree whispers to the land in greeting.*

Arms enfold Bree in a warm embrace. The touch is so gentle, so tender, so familiar. Bree smiles.

"Hello, Emily."

"Hello, Raven Child."

The greeting sings with two voices, flowing in perfect unison. Stepping back, Bree finds herself standing with her aunt and her Ally. Nodding silent greeting to Raven, Bree asks the healing question.

"Emily, you called for me. Have you decided?"

Emily nods. "If it is possible to return in health, I would choose to return to physical life."

"If it is possible..." *The words echo through Bree, drawing her to full understanding. She turns to Raven.*

"The soul has begun to wander and damage has been done," Raven confirms. "But, repair may be possible."

"Please, chiya," Emily pleads. "Will you help me?"

Bree turns to Raven. "May we?"

Black feathers ripple, turning day to night. Bree rises upon silent wings, now stretching, pressing and shifting through the Otherworld. Landscapes flash and roll through her mind as Raven's relentless, dark eyes pierce the Otherworld. Scanning the Wilds, they search.

A flash of light in the distance releases Raven's call. "Crrruck!"

"I see her," Bree replies.

Wings reach to spiral downward, earthward toward the light. Her feet touch earth, and Bree stands in human form again. She is not alone. A woman, thin and elegant despite the heavy, tan and green tartan cloak draped around her, nears the base of a mountain. Her narrow shoulders hold strong under a large, woven bag. A blaze of red crowns her head.

"Emily," Bree whispers.

The woman turns toward Bree. "Raven Child? Is that you? What are you doing here?"

"Looking for you," Bree replies with a smile.

"But, how?" Emily shakes her head, confused. "I am headed Home. This lifetime draws to an end. I have heard the Call and am Returning."

Silently Bree calls to Raven, seeking confirmation. "Has Emily's choice changed? Is this lifetime truly woven to its close for her?"

"No," Raven rasps. "Her choice remains. Continue. Bring her home."

"Are you certain, Aunt? Can you hear the Call still?"

Bree watches as this soul aspect of Emily draws her focus inward, raises her head and ear to listen. Searching through the threads of her soul, she seeks her path. As her chin droops, Bree knows Emily's soul has heard the answer.

"It seems this lifetime is to continue." *Emily's soul aspect looks longingly toward the mountain, then sighs.* "I must return." *Turning away from her destination and the promise of Home, she takes a step, then pauses. Scanning the ground before her, she hesitates.* "But, I have forgotten the way."

Bree smiles. "I know the way, Aunt. Will you let me show you?"

With a nod from this soul aspect of Emily, Bree reaches to take her aunt's hand. Fiery light flashes, and Bree finds herself holding a ball of crimson-gold light. Soul light.

"Crrruck!" *Raven calls approval.*

Black feathers ripple as day turns to night. Bree rises again, the ball of crimson-gold light grasped firmly in her hands.

"Hold tight, Raven Child," *Bree's Ally calls as wings shift and dance in the wind.* "Two more soul parts remain to be retrieved."

JENNIFER LYNN

CHAPTER SEVENTEEN

Light flashes in the distance, blazing into Bree's awareness through Raven's eye. Black-on-white lines branch and root in her vision, as wings the color of midnight reach to stretch across the Otherworld.

"Crrruck!"

Black feathers ripple, pulsing with the currents, shifting to spiral downward, earthward, toward the light. Feet touching earth, Bree rises from a crouch to stand in human form. Oak trees, ancient and watchful, stretch in all directions from the thin, earthen path beneath her. The lowest of their leaf-covered branches towers several yards above her head.

Bree presses her toes into the earth and smiles. She knows this place and the Spirits here. Touching fingertips to lips, she bends down, offers the kiss to the earth.

"Blessed is the Mother," she whispers in greeting. A gentle tremble rushes through her, as the leaves rustle on the trees. Bree bows her head, grateful for the sign of welcome.

Rising to a standing position, Bree looks at the path stretching before her and knows exactly where it leads. A dear old friend, she smiles at the track, certain she could walk it with her eyes closed. She chuckles softly, realizing she and Emily have done just that, in so many lifetimes past.

"Of course she would come here," Bree beams.

"Crrruck! Crrruck! Crrruck!" Raven soars overhead, the shadow of potential, reminding her.

With a silent nod, Bree walks along the path, following it as it bends sunwise. As always, her breath catches as the western edge of the ancient grove rises suddenly into view. Sunlight streams from the natural clearing to spill through the oak trees, bathing her tenderly in the light of the nemeton. Bowing her head before that sacred space, Bree opens her arms and lifts her palms to drink in the light.

A rustling in the tree ahead of her draws Bree's attention, as Raven shifts position. "Look, Raven Child," *her Ally prompts and turns toward the clearing.*

Bree gasps. There, in the center of the oak grove, Emily's soul part sits. Eyes closed, her head bows gently over the acorn resting in her open palm. Light dances all around her, rising up from the earth of the grove and spiraling to encompass her. Her own inner light pulsates, flowing from the depths of her soul outward to swirl and dance with the light from the grove. Pressing palm to palm and bowing slightly, Bree backs quietly away from the circle.

"Grrrruck," *Raven rasps from her perch in the oak tree.* "Why do you delay?"

Bree frowns at her Ally. "To honor her process. Emily is clearly in deep communion with the Spirit of the Grove. I would wait and speak with her when she returns."

Raven shakes her head, clacking her beak. "This part of Emily's soul has lost its tie to her physical body. It lives now beyond any concept of time. Are you prepared to wait forever?"

Bree hesitates, still reluctant to disrupt Emily's sacred communion. Sighing, she relents. "No."

"Good," *Raven chirrups.* "You are known to the Spirits of this place and are welcome here. Enter the circle and seek the Spirit of the Grove yourself."

With a nod of agreement, Bree turns to her left. In the earth before her, water bubbles up and spills to form a small pool. Touching fingertips to lips, she bends down and offers the kiss to the waters.

"Peace be upon the waters. Peace be upon this place. Peace be," *she whispers in greeting. The air around her stills as light dances within the pool.* "Thank you," *she adds, grateful for the welcome.*

Rising to a standing position, Bree finds herself gazing into deep, sea-blue eyes. A woman – radiant, red-haired and ageless – stands before her. With a smile, the woman extends her hand. Removing cloak and chemise, Bree takes her hand and follows her into the pool. Immersed in the sacred waters, Bree leans back, welcoming the ritual cleansing, allowing herself to be bathed – head, body, hands and feet.

Emerging from the pool, Bree re-ties her chemise. The woman steps closer and holds out a chalice, gesturing for Bree to drink. Cool, refreshing liquid spills down her throat, bathing her on the inside. A gentle warmth spreads through her body and she closes her eyes, basking in the blessing.

Opening her eyes, Bree extends the chalice in return. The woman shifts her glance to the cup and it dissolves slowly from view. Folding Bree's cloak over her arm, the woman smiles and gestures Bree onward, toward the nemeton. They walk together, stopping at the entrance to the grove. The woman smiles and steps to the side.

"Go raibh mille maith agaibh," Bree whispers, offering thanks to the Guardian.

On both sides of the entrance, an oak tree reaches and branches into the sky. Standing before them, Bree lets her eyes drift across their trunks, scanning their broad bodies, the scars from lost limbs and lightning strikes – the wisdom of growth earned through countless millennia. Following the length of their torsos skyward, she leans back until the lowest branches drift into view. Reaching with natural grace, each limb stretches to intertwine with the limb of the tree next to it, birthing a living archway.

Gazing into that gateway, Bree senses an awareness reaching to touch her own, a gentle pressure like the touch of a tentative lover. Closing her eyes, Bree welcomes that touch, responds with a soft, energetic caress of her own. Pressing fingertips to lips, she steps into the archway and reaches out to touch the bark, offering a kiss to each tree.

"Peace be upon this place," she whispers the ritual greeting. "Peace be between us..."

"... Now and through all time." Love washes through her with the voice of the Grove, setting her soul aglow.

Bowing her head to honor the welcoming and with feet bared to kiss the earth, Bree enters the ancient Grove. With each step, her feet sink slightly into the ancient moss, the layers of leaves and undergrowth from millennia grounding her with its living carpet. The light of the Grove floods through Bree, bathing her – mind, body and soul – in radiance. Her energy being tingles, and she exhales.

Bree steps into the center of the circle and settles onto the moss, placing herself face to face with her aunt. Palms pressing softly upon the earth, Bree closes her eyes and calls to the Spirit of the Grove.

"Peace be upon you, Ancient One."

"And upon you." *Green eyes open to drift in Bree's awareness.* "Welcome, chiya," *The Spirit of the Grove greets her in a voice neither male nor female and lush as the earth.* "Why come you to this place?"

Opening her eyes, Bree shifts her focus onto her aunt, as her soul whispers one word... "Emily."

Light pours from Bree, spilling into that word the truth in snap-shot images... Emily frail and withering in the hospital bed... Emily pleading for healing... Bree and Raven searching the Otherworld for wandering soul parts... Raven instructing Bree to enter the nemeton... Bree seated in the grove, bowing in appeal.

Soft and gentle, understanding washes over Bree, shifts to sorrow and yields into compassion.

"She will not hear you," *the Spirit of the Grove answers through blinking, green eyes.* "She seeks now only the Mystery."

Bree smiles, replying softly, "As she has always done." *Again, Bree offers images in response... shapes of Emily's soul from lifetimes past – a Druid priestess, an Oracle of Delphi, a Daughter of Isis... and moments from this lifetime – Emily with Rose and Bree gathered in the family grove, Emily alone, eyes closed in vision.*

Green eyes drift before her, blinking slowly. "She will not hear you."

"I understand her passion and her desire to seek," Bree continues, *images flowing from her own lifetime as she speaks... Bree drumming, eyes closed before her altar for Working... sitting with clients... holding three-month-old Fiona in the family grove.* "She shared it with me. She helped me to hear the Mystery calling me. That calling informs my life, guides my every step through the physical world, the Otherworld and all of the spaces in between. Now, that calling carries me here, to you and to Emily."

"She will not hear you," *the Spirit of the Grove insists through unyielding, green eyes.*

Bree sighs. Uncertainty wells within her, eroding her confidence. "Did I misunderstand," *she wonders quietly.*

"The self must be present to be transformed." *Raven's voice rasps through the Grove.* "Emily has chosen. She calls her soul part to return. Only then may life continue."

Bree focuses again on Emily's plea for healing. "Spirit of the Grove, I come at Emily's request, on behalf of her soul. Please, will you help me? Will you carry my message to her soul part within the grove?"

Green eyes drift through Bree's awareness, blinking slowly. As the lids drop to slits, light blazes – verdant and translucent –

cascading to shower as sparks around Bree before disappearing from view.

"Wait, Raven Child..." Raven's voice echoes through Bree. "Wait, and hold Emily's request for healing in your heart."

Nodding, Bree opens her eyes. Light ripples and pulses through the Grove, shimmering translucent green as it flows from the edges to pool around Emily at the center. Closing her eyes, Bree offers a silent 'thank you' to the Spirit of the Grove before turning her focus back to Emily.

"The self must be present to be transformed," Bree echoes Raven's wisdom.

With a soft exhale, Bree slows her breathing, then lets her mind drift back, through the threads of experience, to the moment of Emily's choice. Red hair flames before her eyes, as words rise into awareness... "If it is possible to return in health, I would choose to return to physical life"... "Please, chiya. Will you help me?"... Sending her awareness into the deep silence of that sacred space, Bree lets the vibration of that plea flow.

Further and further the ache ripples, stretching to reach the edge of the circle and pooling to fill the nemeton. Spiraling in upon itself, the vibration of Emily's appeal echoes, ringing against the trees themselves.

That ache whirling around her and ruffling her hair, Bree presses her eyes closed and wills herself to hold the focus. She sees only Emily's red hair, hears only the words of her plea... "Please, chiya..."

Silence stretches again through the grove. Opening her eyes, Bree stares into bright, clear hazel eyes. Acorn gone from her hand, Emily's soul part sits, smiling, palms folded in her lap. Radiant light flows lovingly through the grove.

With a nod, Emily rises and extends a hand to Bree. "I will go with you, Raven Child. Will you show me the way?"

"I will," Bree replies, standing.

Reaching to take her aunt's hand, fiery light flashes and Bree finds herself, once again, with a ball of crimson-gold light – soul light – pulsing in her hands. Slightly larger, this ball shines more brightly, gleaming with the radiance of two soul parts.

"Crrruck!" Raven calls approval.

Feathers the color of midnight ripple as day turns to night. Bree rises again, the ball of crimson-gold light grasped firmly in her hands.

"Hold tight, Raven Child," Bree's Ally calls as wings shift and dance in the wind. "One more soul part remains to be retrieved."

CHAPTER EIGHTEEN

Black feathers dance and stream on the wind, as Bree sails upon silent wings, pressing and stretching through the Otherworld. Landscapes flash and roll through her mind as Raven's relentless, dark eyes pierce the Otherworld. Scanning... hunting... searching for soul light.

Wings pull, tense and strain, banking against the currents, spiraling to stretch anew. Still searching...

Feathers slack, dropping toward the right, shifting to spiral downward, earthward. A flash of light in the distance sparks through Raven's eye, glinting across Bree's awareness. Feet touching earth, Bree rises to stand in human form again.

Hairy green stems grow like beanstalks all around her, casting out leaves as large as Bree's head. Lifting her gaze to trace the stems, she gapes as the underside of an enormous sunflower drapes overhead.

"Otherworldly Wild..." she whispers to the flower that could shelter two of her. Shifting her gaze, she realizes the sunflower is not alone. A sea of green, yellow and orange flows in giant circles as far as she can see.

"Crrruck! Crrruck! Crrruck!" Raven croaks, her voice calling from within the sunflower forest.

"Coming," Bree replies, as she turns to follow the call.

Avoiding the thorn-like hairs on the stems, Bree walks in the open spaces between flowers. She follows her Ally's lead through the deep, green-tinted darkness stretching out before her.

"I don't see her, Raven," Bree calls, seeking assistance.

Light flares in her eyes, as Raven's vision overlaps with hers. In a blink, the darkness vanishes into a sea of drifting light. Scanning the way ahead, crimson-gold light blurs for an instant across Bree's view, then vanishes.

"She is hiding," Raven rasps.

"How do I draw her out?"

"Show her," Raven chirrups. *"Let her hear Emily's request."*

Bree nods, shifts to stand with her feet apart slightly, her arms lifted from her sides, palms open and clearly visible. With an exhale, Bree begins.

"Peace be upon this place..."

Slowing her breathing, Bree lets her mind drift, just as she did in the Grove, back to the moment of Emily's choice. As red hair flames before her eyes, she calls to the hiding soul part.

"I know you are there and can hear me. I come in Peace, at the request of Emily and on behalf of your soul. If you will listen, you can see the truth of this for yourself."

Something shivers in the distance, telling Bree her message was received.

Holding the image of Emily in her heart, she allows the words to rise, sends them streaming into that space... "If it is possible to return in health, I would choose to return to physical life"... "Please, chiya. Will you help me"... "Will you show me the way?"

"Raven Child."

Barely a whisper, the words flow to Bree through the darkness. Opening her eyes, a faint light, crimson-gold, flickers in the distance. She waits, allowing Emily's soul part space to choose.

"It is so easy here, to live in the light of Love."

Bree sighs, understanding the unspoken message. Emily's soul part would choose to remain in the beauty and grace of the Otherworld. She wants to live in the Wildness, to dance as pure light once again. Bree knows that desire well, having faced it herself on many occasions. Her heart aches as compassion flows through her.

"Every flame must be tended..." *The voice of Bree's mother echoes through her, reminding her.*

Nodding agreement, Bree continues. "The flame, the light, the sacred Lovemaking that is Emily still yearns to live. Without you, she is incomplete. Without you, her flame can no longer be tended. She needs you to continue her dance of Love."

Bree watches as crimson-gold light flickers in the distance, then vanishes. She calls once more. "Emily has chosen life. Will you deny your soul that right?"

Crimson-gold light shimmers and draws slowly nearer, illuminating the forest of stems around Bree. Stepping into the open, Emily's soul part walks forward, stopping in front of her. She stands, gazing into Bree, scrying her energy.

"You speak the truth." She pauses, considering. "Very well, Raven Child. I will honor the choice of my soul. I will return to Emily." Extending her hand toward Bree, she adds, "Tell her, I restore to her the ability to embrace Love easily, no matter the form in which it is gifted."

Bree reaches to take her aunt's hand. Fiery light flashes, and, once again, Bree finds herself holding a ball of crimson-gold light – soul light. Before her eyes, the light of the ball swirls and swells, then morphs into a shining, crimson-gold heart.

CHAPTER NINETEEN

"Crrruck! Crrruck! Crrruck!" Raven calls.

Black feathers ripple as day turns to night. Bree is rising again, the heart-shaped ball of crimson-gold soul light clasped firmly in her hands. Soul parts reclaimed, she knows the journey draws toward completion. As Raven pumps her wings once more, the colors of the Otherworld dance and blur around them.

Swirling spirals flow and pulsate as Raven shifts, stretching wings the color of midnight through the Otherworld. Laughter, joyous and flowing, ripples and cascades to fill Bree's world, as Raven leans into the currents, spirals downward, earthward.

Bree's feet touch solid earth, and she rises, woman once more. Her black hair ripples and dances in the sunlight that seems to radiate from everywhere. Streaks of blue, crimson and gold dance and ripple around her. Laughter peals forth, and Bree turns toward the sound.

"Welcome back, Raven Child." Emily stands before her, red hair ablaze, in a field of wildflowers.

"Hello, Aunt." Bree smiles in return, holds out the heart-shaped ball of crimson-gold soul light. "I have something for

you."

Emily takes a step toward her niece, then hesitates. Uncertainty, sorrow and fear wash over Bree, as Emily closes her eyes and balls hands into fists. Bree yearns to go to her aunt, but she cannot move. She must allow her aunt to choose.

Breathing deeply, Emily breaks the silence. "I choose to trust in Love. I choose to trust in Love. I choose to trust in Love."

Heat flames through Bree's hands as the ball of soul light blazes. Stepping toward the crimson-gold light, Emily spreads her arms wide. With a smile, Bree places the heart of soul light onto Emily's chest and watches as it sinks into her aunt. Crimson-gold light shimmers and flows through Emily, as she folds her hands lovingly over her newly-restored heart.

As the light settles, Emily looks to her feet. There, beneath her, stretches a silver chord – one end attached to Emily, the other disappearing into the distance. The chord, once tattered and frayed, now shimmers with crimson-gold light as it re-weaves itself to wholeness.

"Crrruck!" Raven calls approval, landing to perch upon Emily's shoulder. "The healing that remains must be completed through the body. Only then may life be restored." *Raven turns her head sideways to gaze into Bree's eyes.* "Go, Raven Child, rest a while."

"But, Emily..." *Bree replies, reluctant to leave her aunt wandering in the Otherworld.*

"She is safe, her soul restored to wholeness," *Raven nods from Emily's shoulder.* "Go. I shall remain with her. Come again when you are rested and ready to continue."

Bree stands motionless, unwilling to simply leave.

Emily steps toward her, as Raven teeters and flutters for balance on her shoulder. "It's okay, Bree. I can wait here with Raven." *Smiling and nodding at the field of blue, red and yellow flowers swaying around her, she adds,* "Besides, I would enjoy one more dance among these wildflowers."

"Of course you would," *Bree chuckles.* "Very well. I leave you in Raven's care. Blessings of Peace, Aunt."

"Blessings of Peace," *Emily replies.*

Closing her eyes to the Otherworld, Raven's voice croaks once again through Bree's awareness. "Remember, Raven Child – the healing that remains must be completed through the body."

JENNIFER LYNN

CHAPTER TWENTY

Steam rose from the coffee mug nestled in her hands, as Bree stared into the round eyes of an owl perching quietly in her froth.

It's called foam art, she reminded herself.

The baristas at Salmon Bay Coffee were known for their creamy creativity, but Bree knew this owl represented more than simple decoration. Given her current presence in Seattle and the events of the past twenty-four hours, the image must have been inspired for a reason.

There are no coincidences, she reminded herself. *The Mystery is ever unfolding.* Leaning forward for a closer look, she wondered what the little owl might have come to say.

"Blessings, Owl," she whispered into her cup. "Messenger of the Goddess... What words of wisdom do you carry to me today?"

She lingered a few moments in silence, waiting for a reply, before leaning back in the rattan patio chair. Shaking her head, she chuckled. *Sometimes an owl is just an owl,* she chided herself, then gasped. Chills sent the hairs on her arms and neck to standing, as words reverberated through her.

"Someone is coming."

Catching her breath, Bree sat forward in her chair and looked around her. No one. The coffee house was unusually quiet; even the red room was empty today. And she was the only person on the patio, in This World *and* the Otherworld. Nevertheless, she knew the message spoke Truth. Someone would come. All she needed to do was wait.

Settling back into her chair, she peered again at the foam owl in her mug. "Thank you, Owl," she whispered. "Blessed is the Mother. Blessed is the Mystery."

Bree spotted the almond croissant on the table next to her. She had almost forgotten about it. Breaking off a piece and popping it into her mouth, she closed her eyes and sighed.

"Yum," she muttered through the crumbs. She was hungry. Not only had she missed breakfast with Rose and Fiona, she had Worked through the morning to complete the soul retrieval for Emily. And journeying through the Otherworld always left her ravenous.

She had drooled over the bacon and egg sandwich left for her on Rose's kitchen counter before putting it in the refrigerator. Through the hunger, Raven's voice had echoed clearly in her mind... *"Come again when you are rested."* Bree knew that could mean only one thing – another intense session of Working remained ahead of her.

She had grown accustomed to refraining from food at such times. The more empty her belly, the weaker the pull of the physical body was upon her soul and the easier it was for her to journey. It seemed a fair enough trade... a little, short-lived hunger for greater ease Walking in the Otherworld. The almond croissant would see her through the afternoon. She could eat properly once the healing for Emily was complete.

Heat rushed across Bree, sweeping from the left to right side of her body. Leaning forward, she scanned the patio and yard around her again. No one. She was alone in both This World and the Otherworld. So, why did she feel as if she were being watched?

Her eyes caught those of the owl in her coffee mug, and she heard again the message from the Goddess.

"Someone is coming."

Memories began to flood through Bree, dragging her back to the past, to the last days of her life in Seattle... her uncle's face, eyes closed in prayer hovering a breath's edge from her own, his hands painfully pressing a cross into her forehead as water dripped down her face... Bree and Amber, her first girlfriend, pressed back to back, tensed to fight the men slowly surrounding them... hands forcing Bree's mouth open as her uncle poured something cold and sour down her throat...

"No."

Bree was breathing hard, willing herself to relax. Her senses still heightened from the soul retrieval Work that morning, she hovered on the edge between realities. She could sense her focus beginning to shift, the blurring of awareness that marked the doorway to the Otherworld starting to open. If it opened now, she knew she would slip into the Otherworldly echo of her memories.

"No," she reminded herself. "Those times are past. I am an adult now."

Working to steady her breathing, Bree shifted in the chair, set her coffee mug down carefully, and grasped the edge of the table beside her. *Stay present*, she coached herself, forcing her awareness to flow through her ordinary senses.

Gripping the wooden table, she focused on its solidity, its very *ordinariness*. She could sense its density, pulling her earthward. Exhaling, she allowed that weight to anchor her in the here and now. Her fingers clenched more tightly, pressing into unseen grooves. Keeping her eyes open, she let her mind trace the shape of the indentations.

Her breath came more slowly now, flowing more evenly. Still hovering on the edge between This World and the Otherworld, Bree directed her awareness deeper into the physicality of the table. She set her eyes to tracing the grains and patterns spiraling across its top. She planned to use each curve, like a step on a staircase, to walk herself out of memory and into the present.

Dark lines swirled in jagged semi-circles. Bree realized they marked the growth rings of the tree that gave itself for the wood. Following those arching imprints one by one, she knew that tree had grown with other trees, in a forest – rich, lush and teeming with life. That dark streak, just beside her coffee cup, might have been a knot in the wood. A deep network of roots must have held that tree before it became a wooden table top, here, in Salmon Bay Coffee, with Bree. Pressing her feet firmly upon the wooden floor of the patio, she reached through her inner awareness to her own energetic roots.

Heat rushed anew across Bree's body. Closing her eyes, this time she breathed into the sensation. Flames danced in her inner vision, flickering around her in oranges and reds, then rounding into the shape of footprints.

Tracking fire, Bree thought, recognizing the source of her discomfort. *Owl was right,* Bree acknowledged. *Someone is coming.*

Her eyes shot open as she reached into her messenger bag for her telephone. *He wouldn't*, she told herself. *He wouldn't... Not now...* But, inside, she wondered if her uncle might just try to abduct her again. After all, their meeting at Heather's had been less than friendly.

Better to be safe, she thought, as she typed a text to Rose. "At Salmon Bay Coffee. Check back in ten minutes." She hit send and set the telephone in her lap.

Heat rushed for a third time across Bree's energy field. Allowing herself to settle into the sensation this time, she closed her eyes and began to track the flow.

Shifting to her inner vision, Bree could see the heat rushing toward her like an undulating flame. She sent her awareness walking along the edge of that flame, tracking toward its source. Avoiding contact with the fire itself, she moved at a distance to prevent being detected.

With each step further away from the Otherworldly aspect of her chair on the patio, the blaze softened and yielded into a gentle warmth. As she tracked the fire beyond the yard of the coffee house, the warmth shifted into a suppleness, a dance of light that reminded Bree of the scenting of flowers. A presence hovered beyond that fragrance, within that dance of light. But who was it?

She drew in a deep breath, inhaling the vibration. An image cascaded into her awareness... hills – wind-swept, craggy and covered in purple – basking in soft, summer sunlight.

Bree smiled and bowed in honoring, still careful to remain clear of the flame. After tracking her way back along the course of the flame and across the Otherworldly aspect of the yard, she settled back into herself on the patio. Her awareness re-surfaced to ordinary consciousness, and she opened her eyes, turned toward the approaching presence and waited.

Her gaze focused on the yard, she picked up her telephone and held it in her hand. *Just in case.* She realized she was holding her breath when she exhaled gently and waived as her cousin Heather came into view.

Be careful what you ask for… Bree reminded herself, chuckling slightly as she woke her telephone out of sleep mode. *…It might take you somewhere other than you expect.* Salmon had said those words to her years ago. They were just as true now. She had asked for the message. Her response to it was entirely her own creation.

As her cousine started across the yard toward the patio, Bree tapped out a text message to Rose. "All clear. Heather is here."

CHAPTER TWENTY-ONE

"Are we intruding?"

Heather called from the base of the steps to the patio of Salmon Bay Coffee. She stood, Bree realized, rather *intentionally*. Her arms lifted slightly from her sides, revealing open palms. Her feet were spread evenly on the ground, and she had stopped several feet from the stairs – far enough away to be *energetically* polite.

An image flashed in Bree's awareness... a memory of herself standing in the Otherworld in a very similar manner. Bear had taught her that posture during the first year of her shamanic training. She often used it in her Walkings to assure others – especially those unknown to her – she came in Peace.

There are no coincidences, Bree thought, as she considered her cousine more closely. *The message from Owl, the tracking flame, and now this...* The last time Bree had seen her, Heather still wore her hair in pigtails. *Perhaps she has grown up in more ways than one.*

She let her gaze soften and shifted her focus to Heather's energetic field. Respecting her cousine's right to privacy, she made certain to scry only the exterior, the edges of Heather's energy body and what was readily visible there. Light, golden-purple flashed and rippled around her cousine, arching along the edges of a sphere that enfolded Heather perfectly.

She has some skill. Surprise rippled through Bree. *Is it natural or acquired?*

She sensed Heather's smile before she saw it, as a flash of heat across her energy field. Lifting her gaze to meet her cousine's, Bree watched as Heather bowed her head slightly. With that simple gesture, a wave of gentle radiance cascaded over Bree, and she knew herself to be honored, blessed and respected.

"Are we intruding," Heather repeated as she lifted her head.

"Not at all." Bree gestured for her cousine to join her on the patio. Furrowing her brow, she added, "We?"

"I came with Connor." Heather smiled, walking slowly up the steps. "He's parking the car."

"Of course," Bree nodded.

Watching her cousine settle into the rattan chair next to hers, an image of the girl Heather had been flashed for a moment through Bree's awareness before dissolving into the shape of the woman before her. The wide eyes filled with curiosity were well-hidden, Bree thought, now that the face had rounded to adult size. Strawberry blonde hair still curled around that face, but it swayed at her chin in a bob rather than streaming from pigtails.

Gazing quietly, Bree realized she knew very little about this woman. The tracking fire and perfectly shaped energetic shield made it clear her cousine had achieved a certain level of shamanic skill. Yet, Bree did not recall Emily mentioning Heather had become a trained member of the lineage. As the current first-born daughter and family *Bean feasa,* Bree should have been notified. Would her training have been kept a secret?

The round eyes of the owl in her coffee cup danced through Bree's awareness. *There are no coincidences.* Clearly, the Goddess guided Heather and Bree to this meeting. *So, what is Her purpose? What is She asking me to see?*

Bree let her focus shift back to Heather's energy body. The golden-purple light around her cousine continued to flow evenly, despite Bree's gentle examination.

Either she did not perceive my scrying, Bree thought, *or she has disregarded it. Either way, she is clearly Gifted.*

How deep did those gifts run? Did Heather use her tracking skill alone to find Bree at Salmon Bay Coffee? She could test her cousine here and now, turn the heat of tracking fire upon Heather and see what happened. Or, she could simply ask.

Bree opted for the more neutral approach. "How did you find me?"

"Rose," Heather replied. "She said you'd gone out and thought you might've come here."

Bree narrowed her eyes, considering her cousine. She knew Heather's reply was incomplete. After all, Bree hadn't mentioned the coffee house to Rose until her text message.

She's hiding something. When her cousine remained silent, Bree encouraged her. "And?"

Heather blushed a deep, crimson red, setting the strawberry highlights in her hair to dancing. To Bree's inner vision, the blush rippled as a flash of light through her cousine's energetic field, deepening its purple color and sealing it more tightly. Bree shifted in her chair, intentionally catching and holding Heather's eyes.

She waited, but Heather remained silent.

Okay... Bree thought, still holding her cousine's gaze. *Let's try this another way. Can you see this?* Without saying a word, she re-tuned the vibration of the outer layers of her energetic field until they flowed in precisely the same golden-purple color as Heather's. The gesture was almost imperceptible, but Bree saw Heather's eyes widen slightly.

"Hello!" Connor called from the steps of the coffee house.

Bree sensed the connection with Heather snap. As her cousine turned to greet her brother, a wave of anxious gratitude washed over Bree in backlash. Clearly, Heather was grateful for the interruption.

"Hello, Connor." Bree welcomed the friendly embrace from her cousin as he stepped onto the patio. "Please, join us." She gestured to the rattan chair beside Heather.

"Thanks." Connor lowered himself into the chair.

Once they were all seated, Bree turned to face Heather. "Well?"

Heather turned owlish eyes to Bree. "Well, what?"

"How did you know I was here?" Bree repeated her question from earlier.

"I told you, Rose told me."

"Heather," Bree began, "Rose couldn't have told you. She didn't know I was here."

Heather cast a long glance sideways at Connor. Electricity snapped and jumped before Bree's eyes, crackling silently between the two siblings. She realized they were communicating with each other energetically. Turning back to face Bree, Heather tried again.

"Okay, so Rose didn't *actually* say 'Bree's at Salmon Bay Coffee.'"

"So, what *did* she say?" *She isn't making this easy.* Bree frowned inwardly. *Why?*

Electricity cracked and whined in Bree's awareness as Heather glanced again at Connor, unleashing a flood of questions through Bree's mind. *Do they know they are communicating? Can they hear each other's thoughts? And just how aware is Connor? Is either of them formally trained?*

To Bree's surprise, Connor answered. "Actually, I spoke with Rose. Heather and I were hoping to talk with you, so I rang Rose's house. When no one answered, I rang Rose herself. She said if you weren't at her place, to look for you in Fremont. She said you always liked it here."

Truth... Bree's inner sense whispered to her.

"Okay," she began. "So, Rose mentioned Fremont. How did you track me to the coffee house?"

Bree had chosen her words carefully. In any tradition, mystical or practical, *tracking* was the precise term for the skill Heather had demonstrated. *But, does she know that?*

A gentle shade of red slowly spread its way across Heather's face, confirming Bree's suspicion. In reply, Heather only shrugged and said, "Intuition."

"Intuition," Bree echoed, questioning.

Heather nodded, her composure recovering as the red drained from her face.

Beside her, Connor smiled broadly. "She's really good at finding things."

At last, Bree thought, *an opening for conversation.*

She shifted her tone to the neutral quality she used with clients. "Are you?" As Heather nodded tentatively, Bree decided to embrace the opportunity to learn more about this woman. Silently thanking the Goddess for the gift of this occasion, Bree asked, "Did someone teach you how to find things?"

Heather's brow furrowed, blurring her freckles amidst the wrinkles. "No." The answer sounded tentative, uncertain. With another shrug, Heather added, "No one had to teach me. I've just always known how."

Natural, then... Bree confirmed to herself. *But, she is aware that her ability is unique, or she wouldn't attempt to conceal it. At least she realizes that much.*

Bree's telephone rang, breaking the tenuous thread of connection building between the three cousins. Lifting the telephone off her lap, Bree stared briefly at the name on the display and sighed. Without a word, she switched the setting to silent and placed the telephone on the table unanswered. Her eyes shifted to her cup of coffee. The owl there stared back at her.

Connor broke the silence. "Bree, we both really wanted to speak with you."

Bree shook her head slightly, disengaging herself from the eyes of the owl before replying. "You mentioned that earlier. Why? What did you want to ask me?"

Again, electricity snapped and whined in Bree's awareness as Connor glanced at his sister. Bree watched the energies ripple back and forth between the two, coming to rest finally with Heather. This time Bree was prepared for her cousine to pick up the conversation.

"We…" Heather began, pausing to look to her brother for reassurance. He nodded, even as she squirmed in the rattan chair, her discomfort pulsing like an ache through Bree.

What is it? Bree wondered, finally taking a sip from her coffee.

Heather dropped her gaze to the table. Closing her eyes, she inhaled deeply. With a nod, she looked up at Bree and exhaled. "First, we wanted to apologize for the other night. The dinner party. Neither of us expected it to go that way."

Connor nodded and turned to face Bree as he picked up the conversation. "Honestly, we never intended… We never even thought your uncle would come."

Heather leaned closer. "He usually avoids us."

"At all costs," Connor added.

They are energetic twins, Bree realized suddenly. *Their energies act as perfect compliments to each other. Yet, they are brother and sister.*

This was something new to Bree. She had seen such balance in energy fields before, but mainly in romantic couples. She made a mental note to ask her Allies about such a pairing in siblings, even as she realized the two cousins had stopped talking.

Bree took another sip of coffee and swallowed. "Apology accepted. Now, what did you want to ask me?"

"I told you."

The words rang through Bree's awareness, drawing her focus to Connor. He beamed a crooked grin at his sister. Dropping his chin, he raised his eyebrows before nodding in her direction.

"You lose."

Bree heard the words as clearly as if Connor had spoken them aloud. Heather clearly heard them, too. She frowned and fidgeted uncomfortably, as Connor sat back in his chair and waved his hand, gesturing for her to continue.

With a sigh, Heather leaned closer to Bree and asked, "Why?"

It was Bree's turn to frown. "Why, what?"

"Why does he avoid us?" Heather had found her courage. "Why does he scowl at Aunt Emily? And why does he hate you?"

Bree sighed. She had asked herself that question so many times.

The first few years of college had been the worst. Painfully homesick, she had longed to see her Seattle family. At least once a semester the ache had driven her to purchase plane tickets, but the thought of her uncle had stopped her from boarding every time.

At night, restless and unable to sleep, she had wrestled countless theories about his hatred of her. Clearly, he disapproved of her dating women. He and his priest had all but drowned her in holy water in a futile attempt to excise that choice from her life. But there had to be more. Bree knew it. The endless readings from the Bible and lectures about the life of Jesus, what did he intend with those?

When exactly had she stopped asking herself those questions? Bree could not remember. Staring into the eyes of the foam owl in her coffee cup, she found no new answers. She could ask her Allies, she supposed. But, what would she do with the answer? Did the answer really matter anymore?

No, Bree told herself. *Enough*. She knew better than to start this again. She had chased both theories and questions down enough tunnels and blind alleys to know, in the end, they would leave her frustrated, depressed and staring at dead ends.

Bree looked up into the hopeful gaze of her cousine. *She expects an answer*, Bree realized. *She expects me to know*. Sorrow spilling through her, Bree shook her head. "I wish I could tell you."

"Is it so great a secret?" Connor leaned forward in his chair, his eyes wide with anticipation.

"No," Bree began. "What I meant was, I really don't know why he dislikes me so. And I have no idea why he might avoid the two of you."

Connor turned and stared at his sister. *"Now what?"* Connor's words whined and hissed in Bree's awareness with the electricity dancing between the two siblings.

Leaving them to their conversation, Bree gently drew herself out of their exchange and sighed quietly. In a way, she wished she could answer their question. But she was unwilling to face her uncle, and she knew it.

Bree let her gaze drift from Connor to Heather and back again, as she sat sipping her coffee and considering her cousins. Clearly, they were both Gifted. Why had Emily not trained them more fully? Would they welcome the opportunity to learn?

I must speak with Rose about them... Bree prompted herself, then fell silent.

Something moved off to her left. Shifting her gaze, she spotted a dark bird flying toward her from across the yard. A familiar presence pressed into her awareness as the bird spread its wings and glided to a landing. In a flurry of midnight-black feathers, a raven settled on the white railing directly in front of Bree.

"Crruck!" The raven called, its black eyes firmly upon Bree.

"Hello, Raven." Bree bowed her head respectfully.

"Time to go," the voice of her Raven Ally flowed through her.

Bree nodded to Raven, then turned to find Heather and Connor watching her, eyes wide. She smiled, set her coffee cup on the table and rose.

"My apologies," Bree picked up her telephone. "I must go." Reaching for her messenger bag, she added, "My Work calls."

Heather and Connor shifted quickly to their feet. Their mouths opened and closed but they said nothing.

"Bye," Heather managed finally.

"Bye," Bree replied before walking down the steps to the yard. Behind her, feathers swished into flight as the raven escorted her to her car.

JENNIFER LYNN

CHAPTER TWENTY-TWO

"Ready." Rose's voice resonated with the deep, even, flowing tones of trance. Her open eyes gazed beyond focus, seeing through to the Otherworldly aspect of the hospital room. "The wards hold, and I will maintain the invisibility illusion for as long as I can. But remember, normal rounds resume in two hours."

Bree nodded silently. In a working trance herself, she knew her cousine would receive her reply. Like a gentle breeze across her shoulders, the ripple of ascent would flow. The circle set and trusting in Rose to hold the room secure and undisturbed, Bree shifted her focus to Emily.

Despite the soul repair completed that morning, her aunt still lingered, frail and unconscious. *"The healing that remains must be completed through the body,"* Raven had said. Bree had understood the implied meaning – additional healing was required. Nevertheless, she had hoped she might see some small sign of improvement.

Bree slowed her breathing. *Emily*, she whispered. The name of her aunt throbbed and thrummed around her. Allowing herself to sink into that pulsation, Bree shifted the outer layer of her energetic field to match the unique vibration of her aunt. A wave of energy released, flowing gently outward, as Bree established resonance. Knowing herself to be in shamanic alignment with her foster-mother, Bree closed her eyes and waited.

The darkness rippled and swirled in her awareness before drawing into the outline of a set of eyes. As red streaked in fiery waves around them, the eyes blinked peacefully, slowly painting themselves hazel. The remaining darkness shuddered briefly, and a redheaded woman exhaled and turned to stare at Bree. Thin, elegant and wrapped in a heavy, tan and green tartan, Bree knew she had seen the woman before.

The first soul part, Bree reminded herself. Gazing into those hazel eyes, Bree realized this woman carried the majority of Emily's soul for this incarnation. She knew, too, that the soul part had left because of a simple misunderstanding. *What had she said?* Bree tried to remember.

The image of the woman smiled as her words echoed through Bree's awareness: *"...This lifetime draws to an end. I have heard the Call and am Returning..."*

Yes, Bree realized, she had begun the natural transition after physical death back to life as soul.

The woman smiled, then dissolved in a flash of crimson-gold light. Watching that radiance fade, Bree offered a word of gratitude to the woman and the other two soul parts of Emily. Silently, she thanked them for honoring the soul's inherent yearning for wholeness and for following that call home to her foster-mother. Clear hazel eyes rose out of the darkness to gaze across an acorn and into Bree.

Welcome home, Bree whispered as those eyes closed.

Bree could hear Emily breathing in the bed beside her. Slow and shallow, each breath ached with uncertainty, but the rhythm held steady. Bree opened her eyes and leaned toward the unmoving form of her aunt. Scrying more deeply, she could see Emily's silver chord shining and intact.

Good, Bree whispered to herself. *The choice for healing holds.*

A wave of deep, abiding loyalty washed over Bree, flowing with calm, steady strength from Rose. Bree smiled, grateful to have her cousine guarding her back, safekeeping the room and disguising the hospital room door as just another bit of wall to those without eyes to See.

This time Bree had accepted her cousine's offer for a Second. Energetically, hospitals were dirty and chaotic, full of cast-off fears and lingering debris from illnesses, not to mention the wandering dead. Bree knew that better than most. She needed someone to maintain the circle while she focused on Emily. And no one could hold secure space better than Rose.

At ease in the loving support of her cousine, Bree exhaled and closed her eyes. Shifting fully to her inner vision, Bree saw her cousine as a monolith – an enormous, ancient slab of bluestone.

Of course. Bree smiled as she slipped across the Veil into the Otherworld.

JENNIFER LYNN

CHAPTER TWENTY-THREE

"Crrruck!"

Cascades of black swirl and dance, carrying Bree into the Otherworld. The swirling blackness pulsates, morphs into fingers that stretch and reach to birth wings.

"Crrruck!"

With a piercing cry, the darkness coalesces as Raven lands, perching at the foot of Emily's hospital bed.

"Remember, Raven Child, soul and body must work as one for mind to be born and for life to flow in Harmony. Emily's soul waits, willing and ready. Now body must be healed for mind and life to be restored."

Pulled through Raven's eye, Bree sees Emily stretched before her, not as physical flesh and blood, but as a pure, shimmering field of energy.

"The soul inhabits and surrounds the body." Raven hops closer to Emily. "But the body is an energetic field as well. It, too, must be intact to welcome the soul, to shelter the soul, to integrate with soul, lest life force simply spill away."

The remnants of Emily's etheric body fill Bree's vision. Jagged edges, cracks and great rents gape in silent outrage, whispering of an as-yet-unnamed trauma that left Emily's life force uncontained, weeping slowly, silently away.

Bree knows she must ask the healing question. "How did the soul container come to be so damaged, Raven? And how may it be healed?"

Water rushes to flow over Bree, carrying her downward, releasing her into a flowing tide. Scales rub against skin as her body shifts, shrinks, condenses. Breathing now through familiar gills, Bree swims beside Salmon. Along branching rivers and up cascading waterfalls, she glides with her Ally through the waters of the Otherworld. Rising, they ripple the quiet surface of a pond.

Two women walk on the pathway that curls alongside the pond. On one woman, fiery red hair dances, and Bree smiles inwardly.

"Emily," she whispers.

"Yes," Salmon confirms.

The women walk arm in arm, heads leaning in close to share thoughts in whispers. Emily stops, bends to admire a flower in blossom. But the other woman sees only Emily.

"I love you."

Emily turns to face the woman, surprise dancing gently upon her face. Gazing into the eyes of her friend, surprise blossoms into a loving smile. "I love you, too."

The woman smiles and steps closer, reaching to embrace Emily. Leaning into that embrace, Emily's face dances in loving radiance, then cascades to darkness. Abruptly, Emily steps away from the woman, shakes her head.

The two women are talking, but Bree hears only the voice of Salmon. "Emily loves her." *Emily steps away further, shaking her head. With tears spilling down her cheeks, she turns and walks away.* "But she walked away. She refused to embrace Love. She refused Love because she was afraid her family would disapprove."

The other woman stands, watching, as Emily walks away. A deep longing aches through Bree's chest and catches at her breath. She can hear the woman wishing, praying silently for Emily to turn around, to come back to her. As Emily disappears around a corner, the woman sinks slowly to the ground, sobbing.

"Walking away from Love caused Emily's soul container to shatter. This is the source of Emily's coma," *Salmon explains.* "This is the wounding that must be healed."

Bree's heart lurches. Swimming beside Salmon, she asks, "How?"

Light flashes – opalescent radiance blinding her. Scales yield to flesh, and Bree sits on the grass in human form. Beside Bree, Emily sits, eyes etched red from crying, gently stroking the waters of the pond with her fingers.

Again, Bree asks the healing question. "What happened, foster-mother? What made you walk away from Love?"

Emily frowns, tears welling in her eyes. "Fear. I was afraid."

A third time, Bree asks the healing question. "Of what, foster-mother? Of what were you afraid?"

Emily's fingers daub the waters of the pond, releasing ripples across the waters, gently rocking Salmon. A tear slides down Emily's cheek. "Of drowning... I was afraid of drowning in that Love."

Emily's fingers drift upon the waters, softly stroking Salmon.

"I can teach you to swim in the waters of Love," Salmon offers. "If you will let me."

Golden radiance ripples through the waters of the pond as Emily's fingers trace and retrace the length of Salmon. Another tear slides down Emily's cheek and splashes into the pool, sending the golden light to dancing. Shimmering brilliantly, the light rises, tracking its way along Emily's fingers and up her arm. With a flash, the golden brilliance engulfs Emily and disappears into the waters.

Bree remains alone, sitting on the grass beside the pond.

"If it is possible to return in health..." Emily's voice echoes through Bree's awareness, calling her back to her aunt's healing request. Closing her eyes, Bree lets her awareness drift in that choice as red hair flames before her eyes... "Please, chiya. Will you help me?"

Drifting in the vibration of that plea, Bree begins to sway, a gentle, pulsing rhythm rocking her. The pulsation builds inside her, growing, aching, needing... Until needing becomes yearning, longing, crying. Her jaw rocks open, and the crying escapes as a tone. Deep, steady and bold, sound pours through Bree and out into the Otherworld, etching through the ethers Emily's intention to embrace healing.

On and on the tone aches its healing song, filling Bree until it floods her completely. Pressing her eyes more tightly closed, she wills herself to hold the focus. Rocked in the pulsating, Bree hears only the song, the cry for healing flowing.

Silence rises, replacing the tone and leaving Bree empty. Still swaying gently, she gathers her awareness – pulls it back from the ethers and draws it back into her soul body. Opening her eyes, Bree stares into bright, clear, hazel eyes.

With a smile, Emily enfolds Bree in her arms and whispers, "Thank you."

JENNIFER LYNN

CHAPTER TWENTY-FOUR

"Crrruck!"

Raven's call carried Bree out of the Otherworld and back into Emily's hospital room. Opening her eyes to the dual vision of trance, she could see the hospital room overlaid with its Otherworldly aspect.

Midnight-black feathers rustled, drawing Bree's focus. She watched Raven stretch her wings wide and glide into a banking arc. As her Ally approached from the left, Bree wondered where Raven was heading, then her shoulder blazed with the sharp sting of talons gripping. Bree craned her neck to the right to avoid the flurry as Raven settled her feathers around her.

"Comfortable?" Bree asked once her Ally had stopped moving.

Raven tilted her head and blinked gleaming-black eyes, but said nothing.

With Raven perched watchfully on her shoulder, Bree scanned the space. Behind her rose an enormous bluestone. Smiling again at the Otherworldly image, Bree re-tuned her inner awareness to see through the overlay to the physical form beneath it. The monolith rippled and swirled before dissolving into the form of her cousine. She sat comfortably, eyes half-closed and breathing easily. A shimmer of energy flowed from her to enclose the room, confirming what Bree needed to know – Rose continued to hold the circle and the illusion on the door was intact.

Good, Bree sighed.

She knew a clock hung on the wall behind her, but she chose not to turn and look. How much time had elapsed on This Side of the Veil while she was Walking, Bree could not guess. In truth, it did not matter.

"Time is a human construct," her Bear Ally had told her once. *"Time as you know it – as hours passing on a clock – does not exist in the Otherworld. Here, time simply is. Here, everything is now."*

How could that be, Bree had demanded. In response, Bear had touched the surface of a pool of water, releasing a ripple that flowed in a perfect, spiraling circle.

"What you call time, we call perspective. Stand here on this point of the circle and one perception opens before you. Stand over there, and the experience is entirely different. The two points are in constant relationship, but how depends on the shared nature of the events, and the direction in which you seek for an answer."

Not for the first time, Bree wondered if she would ever fully understand Bear's explanation. She had come to see time as pliable, almost stretchable when worked from the Otherside of the Veil. As for how two points from separate and distant lifetimes of one soul could be accessible through one point on the circle... well, Bree was still working to comprehend that. For now, she knew enough to trust her Allies and hold her focus, no matter how *long* the healing session seemed to last. Flowing within the circle, she would inexplicably have enough time.

"Blessed is the Mystery," Bree murmured.

A wave of deep, abiding loyalty washed over Bree, flowing with calm, steady strength from Rose. That her cousine continued to monitor and guard the room undisturbed boded well. For Bree knew, the Work was not quite complete.

Bree adjusted her position in the chair next to Emily's hospital bed. Tottering on her shoulder, Raven chirruped and squawked as feathers smacked the air for balance. Talons pinched softly as Bree watched Raven walk down her arm, chattering in reproach along the way. Perched anew on her wrist, her Ally stared in silent poise.

Stifling a chuckle, Bree bowed her head. "Sorry."

With a shake of the head, Raven caught and held Bree's gaze. Light flashed in Raven's eye and pulsed through to the edge's of Bree's energy field. Dissolving slowly, she slipped silently into the Otherworld.

JENNIFER LYNN

CHAPTER TWENTY-FIVE

"Crrruck!"

Raven calls Bree's focus back to Emily's body and damaged soul container. Crimson-gold light dapples and dances, arcing in rainbows and illuminating from within Emily's etheric body. Colors swirl, transforming the soul container into a ghostly screen, then coalesce to form the image of two women, one crowned with fiery red hair.

"Watch now," the voice of Salmon echoes through Bree.

Emily stands before the other woman. Lifting the woman's face tenderly, Emily wipes the tears from her cheeks. "I love you." She steps closer, strokes the woman's face tenderly. "I love you." Standing close enough to whisper, Emily speaks the healing words for the third time. "I love you."

The woman smiles, interlaces her fingers with Emily's, drawing her even closer. Leaning fully into the embrace, Emily's face dances in loving radiance, welcomes the loving kiss.

Crimson-gold light blazes, engulfing Emily's body. As the brilliance fades, the cracks and rents in Emily's etheric body slowly narrow, seal and disappear completely.

"Crrruck!" With a cry of approval, Raven launches into the air. "The soul container again whole," she sings, "Emily's soul can now return."

Light dissolves to blackness. The wind ripples, lifts Bree's hair to dance and flow. Eyes closing, Bree leans back, arms stretching, releasing to the journey. The wind kisses her, lifts her higher, higher, higher as black feathers now shimmer, pressing, pumping, gliding upon the currents, spiraling... spiraling downward.

Bree's feet touch solid earth, and she rises. Woman again, she stands on Otherworldly soil, black hair settling in the drifting wind. Emily stands before her, Raven by her side.

"Ready, foster-mother?"

Emily nods. "Show me the way."

Silvery light swirls, twining to reveal the silver chord beneath Emily's feet. Now solid and thick, the chord pulsates, crimson-gold brilliance shimmering along its length. Raven chirrups, turning to track the flowing chord. Emily follows Raven and Bree walks behind her.

With each step, the colors of the Otherworld dance and blur around them. Swirling spirals shift from flowing to shaping, gathering toward cohesion. Stepping across the Veil, the world around them snaps into form. Bree, Emily and Raven emerge to stand before the Otherworldly aspect of the hospital.

Emily hesitates. Her eyes drift over the hospital façade, brimming with sorrow. Standing silently beside her aunt, Bree holds healing space, affirming the soul's right to choose, bathing her aunt in love.

"I'm so sorry, Bree."

The words hover, shimmering to translucence, flowing from Emily to enfold Bree in silvery radiance.

"I am so sorry... for what happened all those years ago... for not understanding your way of loving... for bringing you here again...."

Lightning flashes around them, illuminating freeze-frame catches of moments past, snippets Bree thought forgotten, discarded as trash. With a gasp, Bree glimpses the flash of herself – younger, beaten and drugged into unconsciousness – lolling in her uncle's arms as he carries her into the same hospital.

"The hospital... I had forgotten." *Bree's words spill softly to ripple the radiance.*

Emily steps closer to Bree. "I am so sorry. I should have protected you better."

Gazing at her aunt, the lightning flashes etch a series of images in Bree's vision, all of Emily – fighting through to her foster-daughter... carrying Bree out of that same hospital... packing Bree's belongings – all with loving determination etched upon her aunt's face.

Slowly, Bree shakes her head. "You could not have known."

Emily's eyes meet those of Bree. "Can you forgive me?"

All flow slows to stillness around them. All light hovers, dancing only in Raven's watchful eyes.

Bree sighs. "There is nothing to forgive. You honored my soul's right to choose. You came for me when you could. You loved me, foster-mother."

"I love you still," Emily breathes.

Bree smiles and steps closer, enfolding her aunt in her arms. "I love you, too."

Lightning flashes, flooding from Raven's eyes to cascade in streaming prisms, flowing, encompassing and absorbing both Bree and Emily.

"Crrruck!"

The light shimmers, pulsates and disperses, leaving Bree and Emily standing side by side at the foot of the hospital bed. Emily's body lies unconscious, waiting. Shuffling beside Emily's still form, Raven gazes at Emily and chirrups.

Emily nods, walks toward her body, then steps into her sleeping form.

CHAPTER TWENTY-SIX

"She has chosen."

Bree's voice rasped in her throat. The sound startled her, booming harshly through her after the silence of the circle. The Work completed and wards released, she sat resting with Rose on the small sofa in Emily's hospital room. Sipping the honeyed almond milk her cousine had brought from home to restore them, the two women gazed silently at Emily's still-unconscious body. Bree waited for her cousine to respond, but Rose said nothing.

A gnawing ache tugged at Bree, setting her to sway gently. Placing her feet more firmly underneath her, she shifted her inner awareness to follow the pull, seeking its source.

In her inner eye, light danced in the shape of a rope, floating between Rose and Emily. Bree watched her cousine grab the rope with Otherworldly hands and stretch it back toward herself. As Rose pulled, Bree listed with another tug. Then her cousine dropped the rope. As it fell slack, Bree swayed gently once more. The ache pulsed through her anew, and Bree understood – Rose's yearning, her desire for her mother to return to physical life, was competing with her need to honor her mother's choice... whatever that choice might be.

Glancing up at her cousine, Bree waited. But Rose said nothing.

Rose had heard Bree. Bree knew that to be true. She also knew, despite her cousine's silence, Rose wanted – even needed – to hear Emily's answer. But for Rose, at that moment, the question was beyond asking.

"In the sacred dance of co-creation human beings hold the gift of choice..." Emily's voice drifted to Bree from her childhood. Awareness blurring gently, Bree was a girl again. Seated beside Rose on her aunt's couch with feet dangling in home-woven, wool socks, Bree looked up into the loving face of her aunt.

"As souls, we enter every lifetime with a purpose – a list of experiences to be had, energies to cultivate, tasks to complete. Each soul is free to choose how it walks through a given lifetime – how it denies, acknowledges or completes its purpose. For only a soul can know what choice upholds its purpose, maintains its integrity and cultivates authenticity. And every soul has the right to create its own experience."

Looking down at her feet, wool socks darkened and thickened into black, leather boots. An adult again, Bree glanced at her aunt's still form as Emily's voice echoed once more.

"Choice is a sacred right, and a soul's choice *must* be honored."

How many times had Emily repeated those words to them? How many times had Bree repeated those words to students, clients, the loved ones of her patients? Those words had become a mantra for Bree, a sacred prayer etched lovingly along the borders of her energetic body, a guiding principle for her Work and her soul.

Like Bree, Rose honored the sacredness of choice. Bree knew that well. She remembered her cousine's sheltering support, gifted in those turbulent, final days in Seattle. And, for years, living in separate cities, Bree had heard the sorrow aching behind her cousine's smiles as Bree repeatedly declined invitations to visit Seattle.

"You know I must ask, cousine," Rose would clarify but never complain.

Bree had understood. Emily had taught them that Truth, too... "The question must be asked for the door to healing to open, and the soul's choice must be honored. Always."

Here, now, they had worked together to ask the healing question and to honor Emily's choice. And Rose needed to know.

Bree started again. "She has chosen, cousine."

That gnawing ache tugged again at Bree, then sharpened, stabbing her hotly. Wincing, she saw Rose close her eyes, drop her chin and stiffen, before breathing in deeply. Electricity crackling along her skin, Bree sensed her cousine's energetic boundary firming.

She expects the worst, Bree realized.

"No," Salmon's loving voice corrected. *"She shields against the worst while holding space for the best. It is her strength. Now, tell her."*

"Cousine..." Bree's voice flowed gently, a healing balm of loving compassion. "Rose... Emily has chosen to return to this life."

Sparks sizzled in her awareness as Bree sensed the message filter through the warding around Rose's energetic field and blossom into understanding.

Exhaling slowly, Rose turned to face Bree and opened watery eyes. "How long? How long before she wakes?"

The energy of the room rippled and tensed. Following the shift, Bree turned her focus to the now-opening door. Dr. Walters, Emily's Attending, stood in the doorway. Bree watched as he glanced toward the bed and nodded, his expectation showing outwardly.

Bree broke the silence. "Hello, doctor."

Dr. Walters turned and smiled. "Rose... Dr. MacLeod..." With a broadening smile and welcoming handshake, Dr. Walters greeted both women. "The nurses mentioned you were here." Gesturing toward Emily, he focused on Bree. "Well, what do you think?"

"She will awaken within forty-eight hours."

Dr. Walters stared at Bree. He turned, scanned Emily's unconscious form in the bed with doubting eyes. Shaking his head, he returned his focus to Bree. "Dr. MacLeod," he began, "that isn't very likely. The chart indicates no change in Emily's condition."

Rose stepped into the conversation. "If Bree says Emily will awaken, then Emily *will* awaken."

Dr. Walters shook his head. "Rose, please, you cannot get your hopes up like that."

But Rose stood firm, certainty etched in the set of her face and shoulders.

"Dr. MacLeod, please..." Dr. Walters pleaded.

But Bree *knew*. In her inner eye she could already see soul light gathering within Emily's soul container. She could sense the pulsation building, the thrumming flow of life uniting mind, body and soul. Within two days, Bree knew Emily's life force would shine crimson-gold on this side of the Veil.

"She will awaken within forty-eight hours."

Dr. Walters stood gaping at Bree, unable to believe his eyes and ears. She had seen it before... colleagues, attending physicians gawking in disbelief, insisting that Bree was wrong, only to see Bree proven right. Nothing could be said to change Dr. Walters' mind. He would have to see it for himself. Understanding that, Bree remained silent.

Rose walked over to the bed and stood holding Emily's hand.

Exasperated with Bree's lack of response, Dr. Walters turned to Rose. "Please," he began to counter, "Rose, you cannot believe..."

His words drifted into background noise as Bree disengaged. She had done the Work. Emily had chosen, Bree had offered healing that upheld that choice, and Raven had guided Emily safely back to her body on this side of the Veil. All that remained was to wait while Emily's soul completed her journey and reintegrated with her body.

Raven will see to that, Bree reminded herself. For now, her work here was done.

Rose and Dr. Walters started to argue. One glance at her cousine told Bree that Rose was prepared to handle the doctor on her own. But this was Bree's domain. She had the needed authority to quiet the doctor. As Dr. Walters repeated his doubts, Bree spoke clearly and firmly.

"Then, we shall see. In forty-eight hours, we shall all know what exactly is possible. Won't we, Dr. Walters?"

It wasn't really a question. Bree had prescribed a course of treatment. As a doctor, it was within her authority to do so. And Dr. Walters knew it. He could have fought it, had he reason to believe the prescribed care would injure the patient. But even he had to admit, he had nothing better to suggest. And waiting was what he had prescribed anyway.

Heaving a sigh, Dr. Walters relented. "Fine. Fine. We will wait forty-eight hours and see what happens." Without another word, he turned and stalked out of the room.

Bree was tired. She needed food and rest, and so did Rose. They had done all they could for Emily. What happened next was up to her aunt.

Bree placed a hand gently on Rose's shoulder. "Cousine..."

Rose nodded, placing her hand on top of Bree's. "I know," she sighed, "we both need to eat. A proper meal. Just give me a minute with mother. Please?"

"Of course," Bree replied. "Take your time."

Letting the door to Emily's hospital room close behind her, Bree exhaled and leaned back heavily. Her body ached. She fought the urge to slide down the door, curl into a ball and sleep on the floor.

The Work had taken more effort and focus than Bree had expected. *Why*, she wondered, closing her eyes. She had done Work like this before. Was it her deep love for Emily that made this so much more challenging? Or, perhaps, the close relationship she shared with her aunt and foster-mother? Was it being back in Seattle?

No, her inner voice whispered. It was something else... something deeper... something much more personal. *But, what?*

Too exhausted to try to look more deeply, Bree sighed and opened her eyes. There, but not entirely, the ghostly image of a woman stood gazing tenderly at Bree. Smiling lovingly in return, Bree reached out to draw the woman into her arms. But where fingers should have met skin, only air remained. The woman was gone.

With a mournful sigh, Bree closed her eyes.

JENNIFER LYNN

CHAPTER TWENTY-SEVEN

Bree sat cross-legged on the grass enfolded in a circle of oak trees. Feather-light touches drifted along her body, telling Bree the trees were watching her from their places along the edge of the family grove. She closed her eyes and breathed deeply into their quiet strength.

Images swayed through her awareness... trunks grown dense and sheltered in sturdy bark... roots stretching for miles into fertile earth... branches reaching for the light and intertwining with other branches. She could trace each individual tree, note its knots and unique branch formations, even discern the different patterns in the acorn caps. But, that was not enough. Over the years, the trees had taught her – to fully know a tree, she had to know the circle in which it thrived.

Opening her eyes, Bree let her gaze drift around the grove. Once she had known these trees well. She could have described every bend in their branches, every curl to their roots. But these trees looked like strangers to her. Gone were the familiar crevices and creases.

She sighed. *I suppose I look different, too.*

As a girl, Bree had often been restless. Hounded by what she could only describe as noise, she would flee to the grove to find respite, solace. Allowing the trees to enfold her in stillness, she would find release.

Some things remain the same, Bree mused, pressing her hands upon the earth beneath her.

Sated from a good meal with Rose, Bree had dragged herself to the guest bedroom. Her body had ached for sleep, but every time she had closed her eyes, she woke again. After an hour of tossing and turning, she had gotten up, pulled on her jeans, dragon tee shirt and black fleece, and walked barefoot to the grove. She had hoped to find comfort among her old friends the trees. Instead, the restlessness intensified.

Like an itch that gets worse with scratching, she rued.

Since arriving in the grove, she had been searching within herself for the source of her irritation. Every time she thought she had it cornered, it would disperse, only to reappear somewhere else inside her.

Bree closed her eyes and lifted her face skyward. Moonlight streamed over her, silky and soothing, filling her with tender warmth. *Like a mother's touch*, Bree thought, then smiled. *Like The Mother's touch*, she amended.

Without realizing, she had started rocking, her body swaying back and forth. The moonlight stretched around her, flowing as arms to hold her. A presence gathered before her and she leaned into it, knowing herself held. She was seated in The Mother's lap, head against Her chest, rocking in Her embrace. A tender humming sound washed over her and Bree's body shook. A sob wrenched its way up and out, spilling a cascade of tears.

Each sway of her body summoned another watershed. Exhausted, Bree had nothing left to fight the swell of emotion. The loving song of the The Mother mingled with the moonlight and seeped into her, dissolving the barrier she had hidden behind for so long. Rushing past the broken dam, sorrow wailed. Bree gasped through the onslaught and surrendered to the tide, her sides aching with each pull. Moaning as the next wave emptied her anew, she doubled over and bent her head to the ground.

"Why do you cry, daughter?" A voice – feminine, ancient, loving – washed through Bree's awareness.

Lifting her head and opening her eyes, Bree gazed through a blur of tears. Golden light rippled through her vision as she saw Mother Bríghid now sat to her right. Bree tried to speak, but sobs poured out of her, swallowing any words. Closing her eyes, she drew her arms across her chest and rocked softly as she wept.

Warmth trickled into her, slowly filling the center of her back. Blinking to clear her vision, Bree could see Bríghid's arm disappearing behind her. As the warmth spread deeper into her chest, Bree realized the goddess must have placed a hand behind her heart. Peace wafted through Bree, spilling from her heart out to her head, fingers and toes. With each new wave, the racking eased, until her breath came more easily. Tears continued to spill slowly from her eyes as she found her voice.

"I should have known."

Bríghid said nothing. A gentle silence drifted to hold Bree as the goddess waited, Her hand resting gently upon the back of Bree's heart.

Bree heaved a jagged sigh, tears falling more slowly upon the earth. "I should have known. I should have seen it coming."

"Why?" Bríghid spoke softly.

Bree turned to look the Mother of her bloodline fully in the face. Tears dropped onto her knees. "I should have been able to help her."

"Why?" Bríghid repeated.

Bree trembled. "As a *Bean feasa*..." Bree's voice broke, drowning in unshed sobs.

The silence stretched around Bree, holding her with the golden light now flowing from Bríghid's touch. Bree rocked, arms clenched around her middle, unaware of the healing touch of the goddess.

Bríghid spoke into the silence. *"It wasn't your place."*

The words slapped across Bree's awareness, and she turned to stare in shock. "How can you say that?"

Bríghid shrugged. *"Gwen had chosen."*

Bree stared. Releasing her arms, she placed her left hand on the grass to steady herself as she churned with the chaos whirling through her. Was Mother Bríghid – the goddess of healing, the keeper of the Sacred Flame – really telling Bree nothing could have been done?

Bríghid answered Bree's unspoken question with a question of her own. *"Would you deny a soul the right to create its own experience?"*

"Never," Bree replied.

"Exactly."

Bree's world reeled. She had been trained to be a healer, to recognize and track the patterns and pathways of wounding in order to restore harmony to mind, body and soul. She had learned to recognize the signs of needed change within herself and others. She had even been summoned – against her better instincts – back to Seattle to offer healing to her aunt. But for her girlfriend, the woman she loved and with whom she shared her life, nothing?

Brίghid smiled lovingly. *"Gwen had chosen. It was not about you. It was about her."*

Bree sat staring at Brίghid, her mouth slightly agape. Shaking her head, she whispered, "Are you saying…"

Brίghid smiled tenderly and nodded. *"You would have warned her, intervened."*

"So you prevented me from seeing the Truth. From knowing…" Bree's gaze drifted toward the earth as her mind raced, dazzled in the lightning storm that thrashed within her. Each burst seared through her with shocking intensity, leaving the cool, calm of illumination.

"It was not about you. It was about her."

"I didn't fail her." Bree's voice was barely a whisper.

Brίghid dropped her chin and tilted her face to look directly into Bree's eyes. *"You didn't fail her. You didn't fail Love. And Love never left you."*

The words pounded through Bree, set her heart to hissing in her ears. In each pulse, recognition rolled like thunder. Her soul whispered, *"Truth..."* as somewhere inside her shattered pieces of herself slid back into place.

CHAPTER TWENTY-EIGHT

Bree sat staring at the grass, Bríghid's hand resting on the back of her heart.

I didn't fail Love.

Silently she repeated the words to herself. Her body exhaled as the Truth of that revelation rippled through her. *I didn't fail Love.* The sense of relief deepened as her soul whispered, *Yes.* Then her energy field bristled, resisting.

I didn't fail Love.

She needed to accept the healing balm into her energy body. But, how? Closing her eyes, she called to the trees for their support.

"It is just another season of growth, Raven Child." The trees whispered into her soul. *"Just another ring to mark you. Welcome the shift. Embrace the becoming."*

A twig snapped from the edge of the grove. Startled, Bree opened her eyes and turned as Bríghid's hand slipped gently off her back. Bree could see the outline of a small form wavering in the shadow of the trees. Still in rapport with the spirits of the grove, Bree called to them silently.

Who lurks amongst you?

"A girl child, radiant and fair as the morning sun." The leaves sang around the circle of the grove.

Bree turned back to face Bríghid and found her smiling, her whole being shining with golden radiance and gleaming like summer sunlight.

"Who is she?"

"Fiona," Bríghid breathed. *"Your niece."*

"Fiona?" Bree turned to look at the shadow hovering in the trees. "What is she doing here?"

Concerned for the young girl, alone in the woods so late at night, she pressed her hands upon the earth and started to lift herself to standing. Bríghid's hand on her knee stopped her.

"I called her here."

Bree shook her head softly, confused. "Why?"

Bríghid's face softened. *"She is my daughter. Welcome her to the circle."*

She is my daughter... The words echoed and pulsed through Bree. She knew a deeper meaning flowed within those words. Bríghid was claiming Fiona.

"Your daughter? I thought only one of us at a time carried Your gift."

"It is true," Bríghid nodded, her eyes closing briefly.

"How can You claim us both?"

Bree was genuinely confused. She actually liked the idea of sharing the role of *Bean feasa* with another living member of the family. But it went against everything her mother and Emily had told her. And Fiona was so young.

"Tell me, mo Ghrá, my Love… if you birth no daughter, who will carry my Gift after you?"

Bree dropped her gaze to the grass. Bríghid was right, of course. Bree could hear the Truth of Her words whispering with the wind through the leaves of the grove. She was nearing thirty years old and remained childless. Moreover, she had no desire to bear a child, much less raise one. But the bloodline must be preserved. The Daughters of Bríghid must continue.

"This is not the first time," Bríghid continued beside her. *"More than once another daughter of mine left This World without a daughter to follow her."*

Bree turned to look Bríghid in the face. It seemed strange to hear she might not be the first to choose a childless life. She never stopped to wonder why or how others had ended their lives so.

"It is not important that you birth a child, only that you have one to follow you."

Opalescent light blazed in Bree's inner vision, etching her bloodline through layer upon layer of women's names and interconnecting lines. As her branch of the family tree unfolded before her, Bree watched the shimmering engrave the names of generation after generation, until her mother's name shone, and then her own. This was her lineage, the first-born daughters of Bríghid.

But what if that line should end? How would the Gift, the blessing of Bríghid flow? As if in response, the light illuminating her name dimmed and tracked back up the tree to Bríde's name. As her mother's name fell dark, Bree watched the light as it flowed to the right and etched a new name.

She smiled. *Of course.* The Gift would flow to the nearest lineage, that of Bríde's sister. Bree followed the light as it inscribed lines and names linking daughter to daughter through that branch of the tree – Emily... Rose... Fiona.

"How do you know she will agree?" Bree wondered.

Bríghid smiled and laughed softly. *"She is here."*

Bree gazed toward the shadow in the woods, the small form of her niece. Bree's vision blurred as her inner eye filled with the image of her three-month-old niece resting in her arms as Bree and Mother Bríghid had blessed and named her. She saw the child bathed in light as Bree had held her up to Moon, Sun and Star.

Eight years... that was eight years ago, Bree marveled.

The light blazed and swirled, flowing now as Fiona's hair while she turned circles in her mother's kitchen.

And that was only yesterday. Is she really ready to enter the circle? Can she even understand what that means?

"You were younger still..."

Bríghid's voice pulled Bree to her. Gazing into the eyes of the goddess, the grove fell away as the boundary between This World and the Otherworld blurred. A great river flowed around

Bree, carrying her upon the waters of memory – Bríghid's memory.

"Can you remember?" The goddess's voice wafted through Bree as she drifted further back along the waters. *"I can."*

Light danced across the waters, running with the tide toward Bree. A flash flooded through her, turning her vision white. Shadows drifted against that screen of light, then deepened to form shapes. As colors streaked through the images, Bree saw herself as a young girl, hair in pigtails, barefoot and following a song of golden light through the woods.

Her young face had stretched into a smile, her heart pounding with joy as she had bounded along the Otherworldly gleam as quickly as her short legs would carry her. The golden light had flooded ahead of her, swirling back on itself to birth an enormous lake. Standing at the edge of that pooling, young Bree had laughed with delight. The sound had splashed through the radiance, dispersing it to reveal the family grove. Young Bree had watched as her mother, Bríde, had turned from her seat in the center of the grove to look toward the sound, her eyes filling with surprise. Bree had smiled, for just beyond her mother another woman – ancient yet youthful – opened welcoming arms to her.

"My fifth birthday…" Golden light flashed through Bree's awareness. Colors streamed from the edges of her vision, restoring Bree to the family grove. Bríghid sat beside her, nodding.

Leaves rustled anew from the edge of the grove. Bree understood. Bríghid had called Fiona through vision. If the girl could follow the trail to the grove, she was old enough to enter. So, Fiona had chosen. Just as Bree had, all those years ago. Now, she stood on the edge of the circle, waiting.

Warmth spread through Bree as Bríghid placed her hand upon Bree's knee. *"She is my daughter. Go. Welcome her to the circle."*

Bree pressed her hands upon the earth and lifted herself to standing. Crossing toward the grove's edge, she wondered suddenly, *What will Rose say?*

As she drew closer, Bree could see Fiona's red hair shimmering in the moonlight. The girl stood calm and quiet in the darkness and wild of the woods at night.

That bodes well. She will need that sense of confidence.

Bree stopped a few feet from the grove's edge. Standing with feet apart and facing the woods, she balled her hands into fists and placed them firmly upon her hips. Words flowed through her, ancient and formal, and she pitched her voice deep.

"Who comes?"

Leaves rustled beyond the perimeter, then a girl's voice called, high-pitched and steady. "Fiona, a child of the Love of Bríghid."

Excellent answer, Bree admitted. "How come you to this circle?"

Moonlight dappled, running along Fiona's hair as Bree watched the girl's head shift downward, then level again.

"By the light and song of the goddess Bríghid." Fiona replied.

Two for two, Bree noted. A warmth began to build inside her, like a flame flushing to life. One more question remained.

"Why seek you entry to this circle?"

Fiona's voice called clear and airy. "To live in the Light and the Love of Bríghid."

Heat surged through Bree, bursting with golden radiance as Bríghid's voice echoed. *"Welcome her, mo Ghrá. Welcome her to the circle."*

Bree relaxed her hands to her sides and opened her palms. Stepping back with her right foot, she drew her right arm back, opening her stance in a gesture of welcome for her niece.

"Then in the Light and Love of Bríghid, enter Fiona, child of the Love of Bríghid."

Fiona's body shifted forward through the dappling shadows of the woods. As she stepped across the edge and into the fullness of the circle, Bree saw her niece flame with radiance, outlined in moonlight. In her hands, Bree saw the girl carried an unlit tea candle inside a glass globe.

"Light the candle with me, mo Ghrá," Bríghid whispered into Bree's ear. The goddess stood directly behind Bree.

Bree reached into the inside pocket of her fleece jacket. She carried a lighter there, for her extended wanderings in the woods, and for unexpected moments like these. As she gathered it into her right hand, fiery light poured into her arms. With her inner vision, Bree could see Bríghid's arms stretching to fill her own as the goddess stepped into her. The merge completed, they drew the lighter out and brought it to flame together.

Bree nodded to Fiona, and the girl stepped forward, raising her candle before her with both hands. Flowing with the Love of

Bríghid, Bree reached to light the candle while Bríghid bent forward and kissed the wick. The candle sprang to life. With a smile, Bríghid kissed the girl's brow in blessing.

Speaking as one, Bree and Bríghid completed the ritual. "So be you duly welcomed, Fiona, child of the Love of Bríghid."

The candle danced, sending its light into the grove and holding Fiona rapt. Bree noticed the girl could not look away from the flame. Bree sensed Bríghid stir within her, and found herself bending her knees to crouch at eye level with her niece. Gazing through the flame, Bree's eyes met those of Fiona, as Bríghid spoke through her.

"The flame is creation unfolding. In it Dark and Light dance with Mystery."

The girl's focus shifted onto Bree. *No*, she realized. The girl looked past Bree to see Bríghid, still standing as one with Bree.

A gale of energy swept through Bree as Bríghid rose suddenly to standing, leaving Bree in a crouch. She watched the eyes of her niece rise skyward and back, following the goddess as she stepped fully out of the merging. Dropping her right hand to the earth to steady herself, Bree swayed gently as Bríghid exited.

"Blessed is the Mystery," Bree whispered.

When Bree looked up again, a smile stretched across Fiona's face, illuminating the girl with golden delight. Shifting the candle to her left hand, the girl stepped around Bree and raised her right arm. Bree watched as her niece placed her right hand in Bríghid's left, and the two – This Worldly and Otherworldly – walked to the center of the family grove.

Bree still crouched near the earth when Brighid looked back over her left shoulder and nodded.

"Join us."

Bree pressed hands to knees and stood, then covered the few steps to the center of the grove with ease. She watched Fiona place her candle in the center of the circle before taking a seat on the grass next to Brighid. Settling herself onto the grass, Bree heard Brighid speaking to Fiona.

"Love is the fundamental vibration. Everything is sacred, born of the Lovemaking of the Mother, Father and Creator, of the sacred fire of life." Brighid gestured toward the candle flame, which to Bree's inner eye swelled and morphed into a single flame burning in an ancient, earthen brazier. Bree wondered silently if her niece could see the brazier, too.

"Everything is sacred," Brighid continued, her eyes focused on Fiona. *"And every flame is sacred. Both this flame..."* the goddess opened her fingers toward the candle flame, then placed her hand over Fiona's heart. *"... and this flame."* The goddess paused, her face turned toward the girl's. She waited, her hand resting on the girl's chest, until Fiona lifted her face to meet Brighid's gaze. *"Tend them both with equal care."*

Brighid gathered Fiona's hands in hers, kissed them, then placed them over the girl's heart. Resting her own hands on top of those of the girl, Brighid smiled. *"Do you understand?"*

Eyes locked on the goddess, Fiona simply nodded.

Brighid turned and smiled at Bree. Golden light blazed through the goddess, radiating outward to fill the grove and everything within it.

Bree vibrated, mind, body and soul. Eddies of golden energy rippled and pulsed through her, bathing her in a love so pure, so compassionate, so *complete*, her soul still trembled to welcome it. Even after all these years.

Closing her eyes, she bowed instinctively... "Blessed is the Mystery."

"Blessed is the Mystery." Fiona's soft voice echoed through the grove.

The leaves rustled, breaking the silence of the circle as they exhaled their whisper around the perimeter of the grove. *"Someone is coming."*

Bree opened her eyes to see a dark bird emerge out of the shadows lurking between the trees. Spreading its wings wide, it turned and banked toward her as a familiar presence pressed into her awareness.

"It is done," her Raven Ally called as she circled over Bree.

"It is done." Bríghid's voice echoed through the grove, and Bree dropped her gaze to look again at the goddess. Bríghid smiled broadly. *"Blessed is the Mystery."*

CHAPTER TWENTY-NINE

The relentless pattering of the rain hammered upon Bree's nerves. She was tired. After seeing Fiona safely back to her room this morning, Bree had fallen onto the bed in Rose's guest room and willed herself to sleep. But her dreams had shouted at her ruthlessly as, over and over again, she tried to explain Bríghid's calling of Fiona to Rose. She had tossed so hard she pulled the sheets off the bed.

"Everything is better with a cup of tea." Her mother's voice whispered through Bree's awareness as she sat on the edge of the bed, contemplating her approach to the conversation.

Glaring at the rain splattering on the window, Bree sighed and decided to take her mother's advice. "A cup of tea it is, then," she muttered as she stood up and pulled on jeans, a black tank top and a black flannel over-shirt.

She walked to Rose's kitchen, filled the kettle with water and placed it on the stove. After lighting the gas burner, she stood staring at the kettle. Her body ached and her head throbbed as the rain pounded through her. As steam began to curl out of the kettle's nose, Bree wondered whether she would prefer it not to boil.

Maybe Rose went out for coffee? Maybe she has gone to the farmer's market and won't be back before lunch? Bree dropped her face into her hands. *Maybe I am ridiculously afraid to tell her the truth?*

Bree winced as the kettle shrieked. She poured the boiling water into the teapot, breathing in the heathery scent of Glengettie Tea. After settling the kettle back on the stove, she covered the teapot with a towel and closed her eyes.

"You're up early." Rose's voice broke through Bree's fatigue.

Bree opened her eyes and grimaced. "I know. Sorry. Hope I didn't wake you."

Rose chuckled, then shook her head. "I've been up for hours."

"That makes two of us," Bree rued. "Actually, I was hoping to talk with you this morning." Gesturing toward the pot of steeping tea, she added, "Join me for a cuppa?"

Rose shrugged. "Sure."

Bree grabbed two mugs from the shelf. Gripping them in her left hand, she lifted the teapot in her right and carried them all to the kitchen table. Rose, already seated in her usual chair, took the mugs from Bree and set them on the table. After pulling off the towel, Bree poured the amber-colored tea into Rose's mug.

Rose closed her eyes and inhaled noisily. "Mmmmmmm... Glengettie Tea."

Pouring a mug of tea for herself, Bree sensed her cousine's eyes upon her. She turned to see Rose staring at her through slits.

"Must be something serious," Rose murmured.

Bree sat down in the chair next to her cousine and sighed deeply. "It is." Closing her eyes, she drew a deep breath, then exhaled slowly. *Allies, show me the way. Help me to find the healing words...*

"This is about Fiona, isn't it?" Rose's voice trembled.

Bree opened her eyes and turned to face her cousine. She did not need to say a word. Rose read it all in one look.

"Bríghid has claimed her." Rose stared at Bree. "You didn't sleep last night because you, and Bríghid, were in the grove with Fiona."

"How did you know?" Bree slowly furrowed her brow and sat considering her cousine. She respected Rose's skills but had never known her to be so aware.

"The candle." Rose nodded slowly, wrapping her hands around her mug of tea. "I saw it in Fiona's bedroom this morning. I went in to check on her after I woke from a dream."

The pupils in Rose's eyes dilated as her gaze lost its focus and turned inward, pulling Bree with it. Light rippled and danced through Bree's awareness as images snapped into view, then faded... Bree seated in the grove... Fiona facing Bree from the woods as Bríghid watched... Fiona and Bríghid sitting side by side, Bríghid's hand upon Fiona's chest... Fiona carrying the lit candle... Fiona standing, arms spread wide, illuminated in golden radiance.

Light flamed anew as Rose's eyes snapped back to focus and caught Bree's gaze. "Bríghid must have sent the dream," Rose pondered. "I think... I think She was trying to explain it to me."

Bree traced the curve of her mug with her fingers as Rose turned to stare into the distance. Still in rapport, Bree could see images from the dream reflecting in her cousine's eyes. Then the light trembled and Rose closed her eyes, cutting off the flow. A shiver rippled through Bree.

What else did Brighid send in that dream, she wondered.

Sipping her tea, she actively drew her awareness back into her own energy field, allowing her cousine some privacy. Bree had the slightest impression of a windstorm – trees bending, branches thrashing, hail pummeling the ground. Slowly, the wail of the wind faded and Bree looked again at Rose.

"Are you okay?"

Her cousine turned to meet Bree's gaze. Her usually smiling face was drawn tight. "I think so," she began, then frowned. "Actually, I feel rather sad."

Good, Bree nodded inwardly. *Let's get it out, deal with it here and now.* "Sad?"

Rose stared at Bree. "Well, yes. If I am honest."

"What about?"

Bree pressed her feet into the hardwood floor and called quietly to the trees for support. *"Just breathe,"* they whispered.

A tear spilled down Rose's cheek. "I would have liked to have been there."

Bree's telephone rang. *Voice mail can get that*, she thought, returning her focus to Rose. Then, a prickling sensation ran up her spine and set her to shivering slightly.

"You'd better answer that," Rose tilted her head toward the sound.

She's right. Bree nodded. With a sigh, she stood up, walked to the counter where she had left her telephone, picked it up and answered it. "Hello?"

A woman's voice drawled on the other end. "Dr. MacLeod?"

"Yes, this is Dr. MacLeod."

"You have a message from Dr. Walters. He asks that you come to the hospital, as soon as possible."

Bree turned to see Rose already rinsing their mugs and putting away the teapot. "I'm on my way."

JENNIFER LYNN

CHAPTER THIRTY

Bree stepped out of the hospital elevator three steps ahead of Rose. As the nurses' station came into view, Bree frowned. The same nurse she had encountered on her first day back in Seattle sat at the desk, talking on the telephone. Bree considered heading straight to Emily's room and avoiding the woman entirely. But she needed to know if Dr. Walters was on the floor.

This should be interesting, she mused.

Bree watched the woman hang up the receiver. Stepping up to the counter, she spoke without waiting to make eye contact. "Dr. Walters sent for me."

"So?" The nurse scowled.

"Is he here?" Bree stifled a frown as a sour taste slowly filled her mouth.

"No." The nurse looked down and started shuffling the papers on her desk.

"Did he leave me any messages?" Bree persisted.

"Who?" Looking up, the nurse regarded Bree as if she had appeared out of thin air.

Bree took a deep breath and pressed her feet more firmly against the floor, rooting her energy and drawing her authority upon herself. "Dr. Walters." She repeated slowly and clearly. *Never thought I would actually wish for my lab coat and name badge.* "He summoned me. Did he leave me any messages?"

The nurse cocked an eyebrow. "No," was all she offered before picking up the pile of papers on her desk and walking down the hall.

Bree watched the nurse disappear around a corner and shook her head. She wondered if she should be grateful the woman left. *At least the sour taste is gone.*

"Come on," she gestured to Rose and headed toward Emily's room. Still in full stride, Bree reached for the door.

"Bree, wait."

Bree's arm trembled at Rose's touch.

"Wait." Her cousine gripped her arm, stopping Bree mid-push.

She turned, resting her shoulder against the door to Emily's hospital room as she regarded her cousine. "What is it?"

"It's just... I just..." Rose stammered, then sighed, dropping her face into her hands. "Please, just give me a minute."

"Of course," Bree reassured her. "Take your time."

Bree's gaze drifted toward the nurses' station. The same nurse was back on the telephone. Bree had no idea when the woman had returned to her desk, or if she had walked away specifically to avoid helping Bree. Not that it mattered.

As a physician and healer, Bree appreciated the policies of non-disclosure protecting patients and their personal information. But, Bree was a doctor. She was even officially listed as a consultant on Emily's case. And Emily's Attending Physician had summoned her. *You would think that might loosen the nurse's lips a little.*

Bree caught a sideways glance from the nurse as she swiveled in her chair. *Nurse Sour*, she thought as her mouth puckered from the taste.

Something moved in her peripheral view and Bree turned to see Rose drop her hands to her sides. Eyes still closed, her cousine straightened, took a slow, deep breath in, then exhaled.

"Okay." Rose opened her eyes to face Bree. "I'm ready when you are."

Bree let her gaze drift across her cousine's energetic field. Reddish-silver light rippled and refracted through her awareness, arching to enfold and protect Rose. Salmon's voice echoed through Bree.

"She shields against the worst while holding space for the best. It is her strength."

"Are you sure?" Bree offered her cousine another minute to settle. She could see tension stiffening her cousine's rising shoulders.

Rose took another deep breath and nodded. Bree noticed the stiffness in her shoulders remained.

"Yes. You can open the door now."

Bree turned and pressed open the door to Emily's hospital room. Stepping to the side, she tilted her head. "After you, cousine." Bree knew what awaited them on the other side of that door. Rose, she realized, was not as sure. *Time to find out.*

Leaning into the door, Bree held it open as she watched her cousine hesitate. Looking into her cousine's anxious eyes, Bree smiled. *Peace*, she whispered mentally, sending a ray of loving light to Rose.

"One step at a time," Bree nudged gently.

Rose nodded and took one step forward before stopping. Reaching her hand to the doorjamb, she steadied herself and took another step, and then another until she stood just inside the doorway.

"Rose?"

Bree smiled at the sound of her aunt's voice.

CHAPTER THIRTY-ONE

"Rose!"

Emily's voice filled Bree's ears and set her soul to smiling.

"Mother!"

Bree watched quietly from the doorway as Rose ran to Emily's bedside and sank into her mother's open arms.

"Mother." Rose's voice caught in her throat.

Bree's throat ached, tightening with unshed grief. At first she thought it was her own, then she realized her cousine was holding back tears.

"My Rose..." Emily's voice soothed. "My Rose, *a stór*," Bree heard her aunt croon as she rocked Rose side to side in her embrace and gently stroked her daughter's hair.

"Mother." The word burst from her cousine as a sob.

Bree saw Rose's body heave. As the ache in her throat released, Bree heard her cousine crying.

"My Rose... My Rose, *a stór*," Emily's voice soothed.

Bree stepped back into the hallway and let the door glide closed. Professionally, Bree preferred to make herself scarce during such intensely personal moments. Reunions involved family members. She would only be in the way.

Of course, this reunion involved her family. Bree touched the closed door with her right hand, considering. *No*, she let her hand fall. *Rose needs this time with her. And Emily isn't going anywhere.*

A sour taste filled her mouth. Bree turned to see the nurse walk past and scowl at her. Frowning slightly, Bree wished she had brought a bottle of water with her. Then she remembered seeing a drinking fountain just down the hall and started walking.

Grateful to rinse her mouth, Bree headed back toward Emily's room. Standing outside the closed door, she pulled out her telephone and typed a quick message to Declan. "Emily is awake!" She copied the text before hitting send, then pasted it in a new message for Heather. Bree paused, considering the message to her younger cousine. With a smile, she added, "Feel free to let the family know," and hit send.

Something tugged at her heart space. Putting her telephone back in her pocket, Bree allowed her awareness to settle into the sensation. In her inner eye, Bree could see a chord of light pulling at her chest and disappearing through the closed door.

Must be my cue.

She pressed gently on the door, opening it a few inches. Leaning closer, Bree heard a series of sniffles, then Rose's still-shaking voice.

"Do you need anything? What can I do? Can I help at all?"

Emily's voice floated to Bree, resonant with returning vitality. "I must thank Bree. Can you call her for me?" After a pause, she added, "Wait, what time is it? I really have no idea."

Rose chuckled. "I can do one better."

Footsteps echoed across the floor, then the door pulled away from Bree's hand. Rose stood smiling at her, tears still drying on her cheeks. She opened the door the rest of the way, stepped aside and gestured for Bree to enter.

Bree stepped into the room and paused just inside the doorway. She watched Emily's expression shift from surprised, to confused, to delighted. As a smile blazed across her aunt's face, Bree walked over and sat next to her on the bed.

The clinician in Bree chattered, making mental notes of her aunt's condition. Emily looked less gaunt and frail now that her soul was once again in residence and illuminating the body. Bree knew it was a trick of the soul light, and she was glad for it.

A few weeks back on solid food will help chase the gauntness away.

Emily's eyes still shined overly bright, but Bree knew that, too, would settle as the integration between mind, body and soul stabilized. Allowing her inner vision to engage, Bree could see Emily's soul container and silver chord shining bright, solid and intact.

Emily reached shaking hands toward Bree, then stopped before touching her. A whisper of uncertainty shivered through Bree as her aunt hesitated.

Perhaps she doubts I am really here, beside her in This World? Bree considered this a moment, watching her aunt's eyes search her tentatively. *After our recent Work together – presuming she remembers it – she could easily wonder if I am gazing at her from the Otherworld.*

Gently, Bree reached out and took her aunt's hands in her own. They seemed so frail and cool to the touch. Folding her hands around her aunt's, Bree held them, letting loving light flow until she could feel warmth spread anew through Emily's hands. Then, with a tender smile, Bree drew her aunt's hands to her chest and placed them over her heart. Resting her hands on top, Bree pressed her aunt's hands against her body.

"You're here." Emily's voice was a whisper. She stared at her hands, resting upon Bree's chest and pressed. The firmness of physical form met her, and Bree heard her aunt gasp. Emily looked up, her face softening and eyes widening with astonishment as she gazed at Bree. "You're really here."

Bree smiled and gently squeezed her aunt's hands, as a tear escaped down her cheek. Emotion swelled through her, filling her throat and swallowing her voice. Was it joy, sorrow, relief? Bree did not know. With a sigh, she just let it flow through her. For sitting here, holding her aunt's hand, all that mattered was the smile slowly spreading across her aunt's face.

Silence stretched around them, for how long, Bree neither knew nor cared. Her aunt was alive, well and fully conscious again. The Work was complete.

Thank you, Bree called mentally to her Allies. *Blessed is the Mother. Blessed is the Mystery.*

"You came." Emily spoke into the silence.

"I had to come."

The words echoed around Bree as she found her voice again. She had fought this summons to Seattle. She had resisted, even resented her Allies calling her here. But, sitting here now with her aunt smiling at her, she was unspeakably grateful.

You were right, I had to come, she acknowledged quietly, and her soul thrummed.

Emily withdrew her hands and enfolded Bree in a deep embrace. "Thank you," she whispered. "Thank you."

JENNIFER LYNN

CHAPTER THIRTY-TWO

"I... I can't... I just can't explain it," Dr. Walters stammered from across Emily's hospital bed.

Bree watched the tall, dapper man gaze at her aunt, then shake his head, as if to refute the evidence of the woman now awake and moving before him. As her aunt smiled up at him, Dr. Walters grimaced and walked to the computer in the corner of the room. From her seat next to Emily, Bree could see him reading and re-reading the notes in her aunt's chart.

She knew he was searching for something, no matter how trivial, to explain her aunt's return to consciousness. A change in body temperature. A fluctuation in blood chemistry. Anything *quantifiable* he could parlay into a rationale. Bree had seen it before. She knew the uncertainty left him deeply irritated, long before the wave of chaffing swept across her skin. As if on cue, the doctor scowled, and Bree dropped her chin to stifle a chuckle.

Of course, an explanation existed. Bree knew that, too. She had been knee-deep in the reason for Emily's restoration since Rose had first contacted her about her aunt.

Bree's vision blurred. She could see herself sitting next to Dr. Walters on the sofa at the end of the room. "The human being is an integrative dance of mind, body and spirit," she explained gently in the vision, her voice echoing those of her Allies. "The body is a gift of the Great Mother, a temporary abode for the soul to indwell for the duration of any given lifetime. The soul flows through and around the body, enfolding it in and animating it with living essence. The mind is born as body and soul connect and integrate. All three – mind, body and spirit – must work together for life to flow. If integration is lost, so, too, is consciousness. To restore consciousness, then, the integration of mind, body and spirit must be restored."

Dr. Walters cleared his throat. Bree blinked and discovered she was sitting on the hospital bed next to Emily. A turn of her head confirmed the doctor still stood scowling over the computer.

Bree considered the vision a moment. Were her Allies really suggesting she should speak so directly with Dr. Walters? *No*, she decided, opting to remain silent. *He wouldn't believe me anyway.*

Watching Dr. Walters scour the more recent pages of notes, Bree wondered if he suspected her involvement. *Maybe that's what he is searching for, some sign of my intervention.* Bree stiffened unconsciously as the doctor shifted his gaze to glance at her.

Clearing his throat again, Dr. Walters approached the bed and turned to face Emily. "I'd like to run a few more tests."

"Of course." Emily smiled, looking up at him.

"You don't mind, Doctor?" Dr. Walters turned steel-grey eyes upon Bree.

Her skin prickled, but Bree managed to smile genuinely. "Not at all." She watched his gaze linger a little too long upon her. *Careful, now*, she thought.

Dr. Walters nodded and turned back to her aunt. "I'll send in the nurse." He started to leave, then hesitated, before offering Emily a smile. "It is wonderful to have you back with us, Emily."

"Thank you, Doctor."

Warmth spread through Bree's body. *He's right*, she thought. Bree had assisted her aunt's return to life on This Side of the Veil, but hearing her voice resounding here was truly wonderful. *The soul's choice, honored and restored.* Bree drew her aunt's hand into her own and gave it a gentle squeeze. *Blessed is the Mystery.*

Dr. Walters crossed the room. With a brief look back, he opened the door and walked out into the hall. To Bree, his steel-grey eyes seemed to hover in midair, quietly accusing her, before vanishing out the door.

"You could tell him, you know."

Emily's voice drew Bree back to the hospital bed. Her eyes bulged slightly at the serious expression on her aunt's face. *She must be joking.*

"Are you really suggesting I explain it to him?" An image of the doctor sitting on the couch with her, his face contorted and glowering, flashed through Bree's awareness.

Emily laughed, and Bree wondered if she had seen the image, too. "He wouldn't understand. Would he?"

Golden light shimmered and rippled on the other side of Emily's hospital bed. With a burst, the light coalesced and Bríghid stood beside them. Bree watched as the mother of their bloodline placed a finger over her lips.

"No," Bree nodded, "he would not."

Emily patted her hand and leaned toward her, a conspiratorial squint to her eyes. "Best keep it between us, then."

Energy pulsed across Bree's back and she turned toward the opening door.

"Look who I found wandering the halls," Rose gestured behind her.

"Declan!" Emily's face beamed as she opened her arms to welcome her son.

Bree stood and stepped away from the bed, clearing a place for Declan. Tears filled her eyes as she watched mother and son reunited in a loving embrace and rocking tenderly, just as she had seen mother and daughter earlier.

"Mother," Declan's voice quavered.

Golden light danced, drawing Bree's gaze back to Bríghid's. The goddess had been standing there, watching their family reunion. *No*, Bree reminded herself. *She has been here through it all.*

As if in response, Bríghid smiled, filling Bree with golden radiance.

"Thank you, Mother," Bree whispered, bowing her head.

"Thank you, mo Ghrá, my Love."

JENNIFER LYNN

CHAPTER THIRTY-THREE

Sunlight danced, sparkling off the glass of lemonade in Bree's hand. Closing her eyes, she lifted her face to drink in the sunshine and smiled. The Goddess, it seemed, had joined the family in celebrating, gifting a brief and unseasonal reprieve from the rain.

Great Mother, blessed is Your Grace.

Laughter drifted through Bree from across the backyard. Opening her eyes, she let her gaze track the delightfully familiar sound across the grass and into the dappled shade of an old apple tree. Beneath its twisting branches, Bree could see Emily standing and smiling with Rose.

From her spot across the yard, Bree watched her cousine raise her glass in a toast. Something shifted under the tree, and Bree saw a dark-haired woman emerge out of the shadows to join Emily. Together, the two women touched Rose's glass with their own.

Bree's gaze drifted to her aunt and the dark-haired woman. *Ciara*, Bree reminded herself. *Her name is Ciara.* With a contented sigh, she realized that Emily and the woman were openly holding hands.

"When you cannot go around, you must go through..." Salmon's voice echoed through Bree's awareness.

Thank you, Salmon, Bree whispered silently. *Thank you for showing me the way.*

Rose walked over and sat down next to Bree, smiling broadly as she watched Emily and Ciara share a brief embrace. "She is here today smiling, openly in love and happy because of you, you know."

Bree turned questioning eyes to her cousine. "I honored her soul's choice, nothing more."

"No," Rose countered gently, "you showed her the way."

Declan slipped his arm around Bree, spilling warmth from her shoulders through her torso as he claimed the seat on her other side. He nodded toward the dark-haired woman with Emily. "Gwen would really like her."

Rose beamed. "She would indeed." Waves of delight bubbled through Bree as Rose turned to face her. "Bree," Rose added, "please give my thanks to Gwen for sparing you on such short notice."

Declan smiled. "No doubt she will be glad to have you home."

"When you cannot go around, you must go through..." Salmon's voice echoed through Bree's awareness.

Bree frowned into her glass of lemonade. *So, Salmon, that's what you meant.*

Her Ally was correct, Bree rued. She knew the truth. She had been hiding from it for months, closeting herself in her mother's cottage in Ireland. But hiding would change nothing. Here, too, the healing way forward was through. Keeping her eyes focused on the sunlight dancing in her glass, Bree summoned the courage to speak the words.

"No," Bree sighed. "I would be the happy one to see Gwen again."

"What do you mean?" Rose touched Bree's knee, wrapping her in a warm blanket of concern. "Did something happen?"

Slowly Bree nodded, her eyes still locked on the sunlight dancing in her lemonade. "Gwen is dead."

"Dead?" Rose voiced the question as waves of shock pounded against Bree's awareness. "How? What happened?"

Images danced across the reflective surface of Bree's lemonade... a woman's laughing eyes suddenly caught in owlish surprise... that same woman falling, in painful, slow-motion detail, crumpling to the ground... Bree's empty hands reaching.

Bree closed her eyes, breathing deeply as the images flooded through her. *No more hiding*. Steadied by training and breath, she let the images flow, let the Truth flood to the corners of her soul.

"Heart attack."

It was all she could say. No matter. Here, at least, words said it all.

The tides within her raged. As her breathing slowed, her world blurred, and Bree slipped into vision.

JENNIFER LYNN

CHAPTER THIRTY-FOUR

A tidal wave rises before Bree, stretching to crest directly above her. Her eyes trace the arc of the hovering waters, and she draws a deep, steadying breath. Light flashes opalescent, illuminating the flow as Truth pours over her, washes through her and reshapes the landscape of her soul.

Sticks and mud churn in the relentless tide as waters, dammed for too long, rush to flow onward, to carry life forward and Bree with it. Breath steadying her, Bree pulls herself to the surface. Waters rush around her, tossing her in endless currents, and Bree feels naked, lost, adrift in a deluge.

"Energy must flow, Raven Child..." Salmon's voice washes through Bree's awareness. "Remember, all life is energy, and all energy must flow."

Caught in an eddy, Bree sinks.

"The foundation of living form, Mind, Body and Soul are energy and must flow in Harmony, united in Their dance for life to flow, both in the Waking World and the Otherworld. The flow is the purpose, the process and the pathway."

Tumbling slowly, Bree churns in the depths. "How?" She calls to her Ally. "How do I embrace the flow?"

Salmon's voice rises with the tide, swirls all around and through her. "Trust in life again, Raven Child. Trust in Love. Let the waters carry you."

"The waters..." A voice – tender, feminine and resonant – glides with the turning tide. "The waters of Love are ever bathing you. The waters nourish you as you gestate in Source, in the womb of the Great Mother. The waters nurture, sustain and replenish you as you journey upon the earth. The waters carry you Home in rebirth. The waters of Love are ever bathing you. In the waters you flow in the Love of the Goddess."

Awash in darkness, Bree drifts.

"The waters of Love are ever bathing you." The voice encourages. "Trust again in Love. Let the waters carry you."

"The Waters of Love..." Salmon's voice stirs the depths, tumbling Bree on the eddy.

Bubbles dance, spilling opalescent light that bathes Bree in memory. She is younger, still a novice and newly swimming with Salmon. Young Bree's voice repeats the teaching. "Love is the fundamental vibration. Energy, life, everything is created in Love, pulsates with Love and is Love in manifestation."

"Life is Love in manifestation..." Bree echoes into the waters, releasing bubbles to shimmer and dance anew.

In their swirling light a woman – full-bodied and heavy breasted – dances, swaying to a sound, ancient and aching. Tears spill from her closed eyes, cascading down her radiant, smiling face.

"The waters of Love," a voice – tender, feminine and resonant – sighs.

"The tears of the Goddess," Bree calls in return.

"The Love of the Goddess," Bree and the ancient voice sing together.

Knowing floods through Bree. "She cries in joy! Not sorrow. Not pain. Not despair. The Goddess cries with Love for the beauty that is creation!"

Opalescent light flashes, illuminating Bree. "Love is the fundamental vibration." Bree calls to the waters, to the ancient voice, to Salmon. "I choose to trust in Love. I choose to trust in life. I choose to flow with the waters Lovingly."

"I trust," Bree whispers. Closing her eyes, she allows her muscles to slacken and releases herself to the waters.

The waters churn around her, roiling and cascading in rivulets away from Bree. Something solid emerges from the depths beneath her, touches her back. Grounding into that solidity and strength, Bree rises to the surface of the waters, carried tenderly, sheltered. Rocking gently upon the easing tide, Bree rests seated in an enormous, opalescent seashell.

"Blessed are the waters. Blessed is Love. Blessed is the Love of the Goddess," Bree exhales in gratitude. Flowing again with ease upon the rocking waters, Bree smiles. "Blessed is the Mystery."

Bree was still rocking. Arms enfolded her as gentle waves of soothing warmth washed over her, caressing her. Rose and Declan pressed their cheeks to hers and drew her in closer.

Tears spilling softly down her cheeks, Bree rocked in their embrace.

Awareness flooded through her. They loved her. Whatever had been, whatever Bree had believed in the past, here and now, Rose and Declan loved her. Wrapped in their arms, Bree knew she could trust in that love. She could rely on that love. She could let that love shelter her again.

I choose to trust in Love, Bree sighed. *I choose to trust in Love. I choose to trust in Love.*

Rose and Declan hugged Bree closer before releasing their embrace.

"Bree," Rose broke the silence. "When did it happen?"

Opening her eyes, Bree paused. There, but not entirely, the ghostly image of a woman stood gazing tenderly at Bree from across the lawn. As Bree looked on in silence the woman smiled softly, then nodded.

"Bree, how long ago did Gwen die?"

"A year ago today," Bree breathed.

Waves of shock, sadness and compassion rippled around Bree. The *Bean feasa* in her wanted to comfort Rose and Declan, to explain more fully, to help them process through the pain. But Bree couldn't. She couldn't take her eyes off the ghostly woman. She knew – it was time to say goodbye.

Peace be upon you, Gwen, and thank you for your love, Bree called silently. *Go in Peace and blessed be.*

Across the lawn, the ghostly woman smiled softly, turned and disappeared into the Otherworld.

JENNIFER LYNN

CHAPTER THIRTY-FIVE

Silence stretched, profound and soothing, through the forest of evergreens. Bree stood and closed her eyes. All around her a current pulsed – deep, even and ancient – expanding and contracting quietly through the woods. An image flooded through Bree, an ancient bellows blowing the breath of life into the land. Exhaling into that sacred pulsation, she let herself drift.

The breath of those ancient trees flowed through her. Each inhale soothed with its caress, bathing her soul in a healing balm, and each exhale sang its ancient lullaby. A deep sense of peace spread from her heart to her fingers and feet, and Bree sighed. Life force flooded up from the earth, through her feet and legs, filling her with Love. Drinking in that nurture, the weariness that had hounded her since her arrival in Seattle eased.

"Breathe and endure..." The pine trees whispered.

Footsteps pattered ahead of her. Bree opened her eyes to see Rose and Fiona dancing a circle around one of the older trees. Their fingers skimmed the bark of its trunk. Each touch released a stream of Love, enfolding the Old One in gentle blessings. As mother and daughter leaned in to place a kiss upon the bark, a breathy sigh wafted through Bree's awareness.

A shiver of delight rippled through her, and Bree knew the tree had welcomed their gift.

Bree walked up and placed her fingertips tenderly upon the weathered bark. Warmth thrummed through her, and she offered the evergreen a kiss of her own.

Blessings of Peace, Ancient One.

"Peace be between us..." The tree whispered.

...Now and through all time. Bree finished the traditional greeting and rested her forehead upon the bark.

"Breathe in life, Raven Child." The ancient voice echoed through her. "Celebrate, and drink in your rebirth."

Energy shivered through her, flowing from her fingertips and feet to meet in her heart. Bree stood, eyes closed, breathing deeply. Slowly, she drank the life force in, grateful for the gift.

Thank you, she whispered silently.

Lifting her forehead from the tree, Bree discovered two sets of eyes watching her. She shrugged. "We are welcomed."

Rose and Fiona stepped away and walked deeper into the forest. Bree glanced back at the tree and stroked it tenderly. *Thank you*, she whispered again, then turned to follow her cousine.

She caught up with Rose as Fiona skipped ahead. "I don't remember this place."

Rose glanced at her, then returned her gaze to the path. "No, you wouldn't. Mother found it after you left, on one of her wanderings."

With her inner eye, Bree could see a light shimmering inside the canvas bag Rose wore slung across her shoulders. She knew the bag contained an offering from Emily, "a token of my gratitude," her foster-mother had said. Emily was still too weak to deliver it herself. When she had insisted that it could not wait for her to grow stronger, Rose had offered to deliver it for her.

Up ahead, Fiona was talking with someone. Bree could see her small mouth moving and her steps shifting to accommodate the presence of another. But the space next to the girl was empty. Curious, Bree allowed her inner vision to engage again. Light glittered and danced, flaring to coalesce into a tall, thin stream of radiance. The beam bent over the girl, then it turned toward Bree.

Eyes, ancient and watchful, swept through Bree. They raked from her head to her toes and back again, rippling her energy field, like fingers walking through her soul. When they found her eyes again, light – gentle and loving – flowed from them to her.

"*Peace,*" they whispered. *"I offer only Peace."*

Bree nodded to the tree spirit. *Peace be between us and upon you, Ancient One.*

"This way." Rose called, drawing Bree's attention to a branching path. "Fiona…"

Light blazed and the young girl giggled before running up ahead of them. Bree realized she was still chattering with the tree spirit as she jumped along the path.

Leaves rustled off to Bree's left. Shifting her gaze, she spotted an owl settling into a sheltered perch. The owl fluttered its wings and stared at Bree as if to say, "Well?"

"Rose," Bree began, eyes still on the owl. "How well do you know Heather and Connor?"

"Well enough," Rose replied.

"Did you know they are Gifted?"

"Gifted?" Rose's voice echoed behind Bree.

She stopped and faced her cousine, standing still on the path amongst the pine trees. "Yes, both of them."

"But," Rose shook her head. "They were never trained."

"So I gathered." Bree stepped closer to her cousine. "They need to be, before their skills grow beyond their ability to manage them."

Rose frowned. "Are you certain? About them being Gifted, I mean."

Bree nodded. "I saw it for myself."

Rose grew still and dropped her eyes to stare at the soil beneath their feet. When she found Bree's eyes again, she had a determined look on her face. "I will speak with them."

"About being trained, properly?"

"You have my word."

Bree sighed gustily. "Thank you, cousine."

They started walking again and Bree turned to look for the owl. From its perch on the tree, the owl blinked slowly, nodding to Bree. Returning the gesture, Bree whispered mentally, *Thank you for reminding me.*

Silence settled between Bree and Rose as they walked deeper into the forest. Green boughs sighed around them, stretching ancient branches into archways over their heads. With each step, roots seemed to grow from Bree's feet, reaching with the pine trees deep into the earth. She could hear again the ancient bellows blowing the breath of life through the woods. Shifting her breathing to match its rhythm, she drank in that sacred pulsation.

Bree followed her cousine along a narrow and turning path. The trees here were younger, and she had to weave around them. Cresting a small hill, Bree spotted a circle of three birch trees. It stood a few yards ahead of her and thrummed with vitality. Bree noticed the branches of the trees grew together, creating a ring of shelter. Looking more closely, she could almost see each tree in the circle reaching intentionally backward to grasp the branches of the other two trees. Bree suspected that circle was her cousine's destination.

"Wait for me here, please. I'll be back shortly."

Bree nodded. "Take your time."

Rose started toward the circle of birch trees, then turned back to Bree. "Keep an eye on Fiona for me?"

"Of course."

Fiona... Bree had almost forgotten about her. The girl had been ahead of them for so long.

Bree looked around and spotted her niece poking a stick into the earth. Bree walked up to see what she was doing and frowned. Fiona had plugged a small, natural spring with the tip of her stick.

"She doesn't understand." Brighid's voice drifted through Bree.

Then she must learn, Bree grimaced.

She crouched down beside her niece and lifted the stick out of the earth, releasing the water to flow. Looking up, she drew breath to speak.

Fiona spoke first. "When you need to talk to Her, how do you find Her?"

Bree paused, considering her niece. "Brighid is everywhere. She is that spring you are poking. She is the morning sunrise. She is the new growth of the trees, and the saplings and plants shooting up out of the earth. She is the green of springtime and the warmth that awakens the season of growth. She is the cow and the milk that offers nurture. She is the hearth fire and the sacred flame. Speak to any of these and She will hear you."

Fiona frowned. "How do you know when She has answered you?"

"Well, that takes some practice." Bree smiled. "You must listen with your whole being... your eyes, your ears, your body and – most especially – your heart. You must learn to hear Her voice whispering through you, like the breeze through the forest. Rest assured, She always answers."

"Always?" Uncertainty glittered in Fiona's eyes.

Bree nodded. "Always." She placed a hand over Fiona's heart. "For She is always with you, right here."

Bree returned her hand to rest on her knee and watched her young niece cover her heart with her own, small hands.

"Can I speak to Her here?" Fiona's voice was a whisper.

"Yes." Bree smiled. "And you can hear Her there, too."

As Bree stood, she noticed Fiona closing her eyes. The young girl grew still and Bree could sense her niece's energy drawing inward. Shifting to her inner vision, Bree saw the light of Fiona's energy field gathering around the girl's heart. It hovered there, until a flutter pulsed through the girl, setting her energy field ablaze. A radiant smile spread across Fiona's face as light – the golden light of Bríghid – pulsed all around and through her.

Connection confirmed. Bree smiled and bowed her head. *Blessed is the Mystery.*

JENNIFER LYNN

CHAPTER THIRTY-SIX

The rain had returned. Bree gazed through the window of Rose's guest bedroom into an endless wall of watery grey.

"The tears of the Goddess," she called to no one in particular.

The waters of Love, the ancient, feminine voice sang back to her.

"The Love of the Goddess," Bree and the ancient voice sang together.

Bree smiled. She could hear it now, singing in the patter of the rain, kissing the earth and all of living life with each splatter, each splotch. Like a wildfire, it blazed through her… the joy of the Goddess, Her unbridled Love for creation, pouring out in sacred offering, blessing the earth.

"Everything –," Bree spoke to the voice, to her Allies and to all who might be listening, "every tree, every forest, every animal including humankind – is bathed in the Love of the Goddess."

Bree's telephone rang, pulling her back to the bedroom. A Seattle number flashed on the display, and she frowned. *Who would that be?* She had added contact information for Declan, Heather and Connor the other day, which meant the caller was not one of them. Bree started to walk away from the nightstand, but something tugged at her.

"It's important," the voice of her Salmon Ally whispered.

"Okay," Bree offered aloud, as she picked up her telephone and pressed answer. "Hello?"

"Dr. MacLeod?"

A man's voice greeted her. The intonation was familiar, and Bree tried to place it. "Yes, this is Dr. MacLeod."

"This is Dr. Walters. Do you have a minute?"

Of course, Bree nodded, then frowned. Doctors do not usually waste their time on telephone calls. If Dr. Walters was calling, he had a good reason. Bree drew a quick breath and sent a beam of opalescent light to seal her energetic field.

"Certainly. How can I help, Doctor?"

Dr. Walters cleared his throat, as a frisson of unease rattled through Bree's awareness. *He's nervous*, she realized. *About what, I wonder?*

"Dr. MacLeod, I owe you an apology."

Bree's eyebrows arched in surprise, and she was glad the doctor could not see her through the telephone.

"I doubted your integrity. I thought you had dosed your aunt with some kind of stimulant, without notifying me or noting it in the record."

Bree pursed her lips. "The blood tests you ordered must show that I did not."

"They do. And..." Dr. Walters paused and sighed roughly. "...And I spoke with your Chief of Residency. He assured me you would never do such a thing. In fact, he spoke very highly of you, marveled at your skills *despite* the oddities in your cases."

A lot of work for nothing, Bree thought, wondering how difficult it must have been for Dr. Walters to gain access to her medical training history and connect with her former Chief. It could be done, of course, if he knew the right people, dropped the right names in the right ears.

The nasal voice of her former Chief drifted through her awareness... "She is an exceptional practitioner, with uncanny instincts and an unusually strong code of ethics. You have accused her wrongly, I assure you. And for that alone, Doctor, you owe her an apology. A *personal* apology..."

Bree shivered and said nothing.

"I'm sorry, Doctor. Truly."

Bree nodded. Outside the window she could hear the rain singing its gentle reminder... *Love, Love, Love...*

"Thank you, Dr. Walters. I appreciate your candor. Apology accepted."

"I wish you and your family the best," Dr. Walters added before ending the call.

Bree returned the telephone to its previous place on the nightstand and stood watching the wall of rain falling beyond the window. So, her former Chief had stood up for her. She shook her head, more than a little amazed.

"The Love of the Goddess," she whispered into the endless pattering. "Blessed is the Mystery."

Bree bowed to the rain then returned to her packing. A small pile of freshly washed clothes waited beside her open suitcase on the bed. She picked her black flannel over-shirt out of the pile and began to fold it.

A knock on the door sounded, and Emily called from the other side of the door. "May I come in?"

Bree smiled. She had known Emily would come. "Of course."

Emily opened the door and stepped into the bedroom. Seeing the open suitcase on the bed, she hesitated. "You're packing."

Bree chuckled. "I leave tomorrow, Aunt. Packing seemed a good idea."

Emily tried to smile, hovering not entirely in nor out of the bedroom. A frisson of nervousness, of anxiety, washed over Bree and pinched her stomach. But it wasn't her own.

Bree put down the shirt she had been folding. Moving to take her aunt's hands in hers, she drew her aunt into the bedroom. "What is it, foster-mother?"

Emily sighed gustily. "I never could hide anything from you."

Bree frowned. "I'm sorry if you ever felt that you needed to."

Releasing Bree's hands, Emily shook her head gently. "No... no... you misunderstand..." Emily lifted her eyes to meet Bree's and started again. "Bree, I owe you an apology."

Bree was confused. She had expected her aunt to thank her again, to offer another round of gratitude for Bree's help in her healing. Instead, her aunt was offering her an apology. Whatever for? "An apology?"

Emily nodded.

A wave of strength and determination flowed through the bedroom, touching Bree's awareness. Could she make this easier for her foster-mother? Was it right for her to try? Beyond the window the rain continued to sing its song of blessing... *Love, Love, Love...* Bree drank in that song, let that Love flow through her, into the bedroom and to her aunt.

"Love is the fundamental vibration of life." Emily started again, her eyes dancing between the rain beyond the window and Bree's eyes. "I have always believed that. Our tradition teaches that all life emerges out of Love, that all life *is* Love in manifestation. Everything is a manifestation of Love, a manifestation of the Sacred Love-Making; therefore, everything is equally Sacred. Masculine, Feminine, Creative, all are equally Sacred, equally Love-filled and equally Love. And as Love is the fundamental vibration, *Loving* is a sacred act – *the* sacred act – in *all* of its manifestations."

Emily's eyes settled to rest finally on Bree's. "I thought I understood. All those years ago, I thought I understood. But I didn't. I couldn't... until now. I didn't realize how hard it was for you, how much it cost you. And I'm sorry."

Memories rose up, wailing out of the darkness, pounding relentlessly at the edges of Bree's awareness. *That is over. That was then,* Bree reminded herself. Here, now she was an adult, safe in Rose's guest bedroom, free to choose without interference.

No more hiding, she reminded herself. Outside the window she could hear the rain singing its gentle reminder... *Love, Love, Love...*

Bree sighed. "You supported me. You freed me after your brother beat me senseless and attempted to have me committed. You honored my choice, even when the family refused to."

"When the family refused to...?" Emily stared at her niece. "Do you believe the family supported him?"

Bree said nothing.

What was there to say? Her uncle had stalked her. He had harassed her openly, had called her an abomination and dragged her to Christian educational meetings for weeks on end. When still Bree refused to change, her uncle had taken it upon himself to "beat the evil" out of her before having her committed. Through it all, no one from the family had *done* anything, or *said* anything.

In the end, only Emily, Rose and Declan had stood by Bree. They had cared for Bree, had nursed and hidden her until she could get safely out of Seattle.

Emily shook her head and stepped closer to Bree. "No, you are wrong. The family never shared his hatred of you."

Bree wanted to yell. She wanted to scream and throw every freestanding object in the room, smashing it all to smithereens. She wanted to rage, to seethe like a great, storming ocean. But she could hear the rain singing… *Love, Love, Love*… She could hear Salmon's voice, echoing out of the past… *Love is the fundamental vibration of life. All life, all healing is born out of Love*… She could hear her own voice, affirming… *I choose to trust in Love… I choose to trust in Love*… She knew it was her turn to choose.

I choose to embrace healing. I choose to trust in Love.

Emily shook her head. "We couldn't change his mind. So set in his beliefs, even knowing you all those years wasn't enough. We could think of nothing else to do but to try to protect you."

Their protection had failed. One week after Emily had carried Bree out of the hospital bruised, drugged and terrified, Bree had acted to preserve herself. She had bought a one-way ticket to Saint Louis, left Seattle and severed all connections. For the second time in this lifetime Bree lost her family.

Emily's eyes filled with tears. "I thought you knew we supported you."

Bree shook her head, tears spilling silently down her cheeks.

Drawing Bree into her arms, Emily whispered, "I'm sorry. I'm so sorry."

Emily drew her in tighter, rocking gently. Bree allowed herself to linger in her aunt's embrace. She had missed her foster-mother… missed her wisdom, her simple strength, and her gentle compassion. She had missed feeling like someone's daughter.

I choose to embrace healing. I choose to trust in Love.

A knock sounded and Bree lifted teary eyes to see Rose standing in the open doorway.

"I'm sorry," Rose stammered. Waving her right hand, she gestured behind her. "But... Bree, some people are here to see you."

Wiping her eyes, Bree stepped out of Emily's arms and turned to face Rose. "This isn't the best time..."

Rose nodded. Bree watched her cousine move awkwardly, shifting her gaze nervously from room to room. The sensation of sand paper chaffed against Bree's skin. Before she could ask who could possibly have her cousine so upset, Rose spoke.

"I'm sorry. I can see that. Of course. But..." Her cousine hesitated, looked out the door into the other room, then back at Bree. "Take your time. I am certain they will wait."

CHAPTER THIRTY-SEVEN

Bree took a deep breath and exhaled slowly. Emily had followed Rose into the other room, offering Bree a private moment to compose herself. She had dried her face, but her body remained shaky. As she looked into the mirror in Rose's guest bedroom, Bree's eyes widened.

Three distinct faces – all her own – stared back at her. Like cellophane overlays, the images rested one on top of the other. Bree closed her eyes and took another steadying breath.

Maybe this is just fatigue?

Her body tensed, as if to say, *You know better than that*, and she grimaced. Opening her eyes, three sets of her own eyes continued to stare at her.

Nope.

She had known it could not be that simple. Not with people waiting for her in the other room. Something more, something deeper was happening here. But, what?

Bree took a breath, preparing herself for trance. *Okay, let's take this one at a time.* Softening her gaze, Bree allowed her focus to drift through the images.

What are you trying to show me? She called to her Allies. *Show me what I need to see.*

Her face in the mirror blurred, the edges sliding and shrinking as the coloring deepened. Bruises, purple and black, pooled to stain her left cheek and swelled around her right eye. Her lip puckered to reveal a newly formed scab. As the image stabilized, the gaze staring back at Bree glistened, overly bright with terror.

The light from that stare shimmered and set her reflection to sliding again. Colors glided, collided and dispersed. Then blue, radiant and gleaming, seeped into view. Snaking and spiraling, it etched itself across the left side of her forehead, down along her nose and across her cheekbone, before it swirled inward, enfolding her left eye in ever-narrowing loops. The eyes that met her now were those of a *Bean feasa* – a shaman, fully trained and secure in her power.

Remember who you are, a voice – feminine, ancient, loving – rippled through her.

Tears slowly filled Bree's eyes, blurring her vision. She blinked, sending them down her cheeks. As she opened her eyes this time, only one gaze awaited her in the mirror. Face pale and puffy from crying, she saw herself as she was today.

Remember who you are, that ancient voice whispered. *And choose Love, always.*

Bree considered the face in the mirror. The bruises had healed, but she knew a tenderness still lingered beneath skin and bone. This visit to Seattle had proven that. Maybe this visit could heal that, too.

Gazing into her reflection, she remembered the blue flame and the spiraling path she had seen it etch upon her face. Lifting her left hand to her forehead, she traced that pattern onto her current face, gliding her index finger gently across the center of her forehead, down the bridge of her nose, over her cheekbone and around her left eye. As her hand fell back to her side, she spoke to the woman in the mirror.

"I choose to embrace healing. I choose to trust in Love."

Her reflection nodded in agreement and Bree smiled.

She stepped away from the mirror and headed toward the open bedroom door. "Okay, time to see who is here."

JENNIFER LYNN

CHAPTER THIRTY-EIGHT

Hushed voices drifted in snippets from the living room. Bree recognized Emily's voice, but the other two were unfamiliar. They were, however, all female. Bree sighed with relief, grateful to be spared another hostile encounter. Then she frowned.

I choose to embrace healing, she reminded herself. *I choose to trust in Love.*

Turning the corner into the den, Bree was surprised to find not two, but three women sitting on the couch sipping tea. Rose and Emily had taken seats in the armchairs nearest the hearth, opposite the women. Two of the visitors were older, one with streaks of grey in fading red hair, the other with beautiful, sliver hair hanging in a thick plait down the center of her back. Puzzled, Bree tried to put names to the faces as they rose to greet her. Seeing the third woman, Bree smiled warmly.

"Hello, Ailene."

Ailene returned the smile, stepping forward to share a brief embrace across the coffee table. "Hello, Bree. It's good to see you again, and so soon."

Bree stepped back and looked around, wondering where to sit. All the seats in the room were currently occupied.

"Here, Bree," Rose called, standing up from the armchair to Bree's left. "You can have my seat, and I will leave you to your conversation."

Bree turned to refuse, but Rose had already left the room. With a shrug, she sat in the empty chair and faced the women.

Ailene gestured toward the other two women on the couch. "We wanted to speak with you."

"You probably don't remember me," the silver-haired woman with the braid took the lead. "My name is Sibeal." She paused, her bright eyes resting on Bree.

Bree searched her memories. She could not match this woman with anyone from her past, although the face seemed familiar. She was certain she had seen the woman somewhere. Bree said nothing, shaking her head slightly, and the woman nodded.

"You were very young." Her eyes dropped toward the floor and she sighed. Looking back at Bree, she added tenderly, "I knew your mother well."

The graying, red-haired woman placed a hand on Sibeal's arm and smiled warmly at the older woman. Then she turned to Bree. "My name is Cara."

Bree furrowed her brow. This woman seemed like a stranger to Bree. She could not recall having met the woman, yet a voice within Bree whispered, *"You should know her."*

As if sensing her puzzlement, Cara shook her head. "We have never met before."

"Cara keeps rather to herself," Ailene smiled. The two women exchanged a look that told Bree Cara's reclusiveness was a familiar joke between the two of them. Cara just shrugged.

Bree considered the women on the couch. They represented three generations of her extended family. Ailene was Bree's age, certainly the youngest of the group. Cara was older, probably from the same generation as Bree's mother. And Sibeal was older still.

Three Crones. The thought came unbidden as the image of three ancient warriors – dressed in full battle leathers, greaves and bracers – shimmered in Bree's inner eye. The word *formidable* echoed through her.

"How can I help?"

"Actually," Cara replied, "we're the ones who should be helping you."

"I don't understand." Bree shook her head.

"We are the Council of Three," Sibeal said.

"The Council of Three?"

Bree had never heard of this Council. She had no idea who sat on it or what its function was, much less how it related to her. Looking from woman to woman, each one just nodded at her. Clearly, they believed she understood.

"What is the Council of Three?"

"Not what," Ailene replied, "But who."

Cara and Sibeal were nodding. Sibeal turned to face Bree and continued. "As for who precisely? We are the three eldest, third-born daughters of the warrior lineage of our family."

Light blazed through Bree's awareness, etching a line of unfamiliar names in fiery trees. Illuminating the lineage of third-born daughters, Bree followed the names through generation after generation, branching ever in threes until highlighting the names of the women seated on the couch before her. As she turned to look at them, she could even see them shining, their auric fields radiating crimson light.

A deep humming, like the sound of a hive, echoed in Bree's ears. The buzzing spilled down her neck, across her shoulders, along her arms, and into her hands. Her body trembled.

"And what does the Council of Three do?"

The three women turned to look at Bree directly. Cara smiled. "We support and protect the current *Bean feasa*."

Bree turned toward Emily. Knitting her eyebrows, Bree jutted her chin in silent questioning.

Emily shook her head. "I have never heard of it before."

Sibeal nodded. "You wouldn't have. Beyond the current *Bean feasa*, we prefer to stay hidden."

"Then why haven't I heard of you?" Bree was genuinely surprised. None of her Allies had ever mentioned this Council to her. Not Brighid, or even her mother.

"We have been rather out of commission," Sibeal replied. She dropped her gaze to her open hands as if looking for something.

"Until now," Cara muttered.

"Why?" Emily's voice broke through the silence.

Sibeal sighed noisily. She rubbed her palms across her knees, then lifted her gaze to Bree. When she spoke, her voice sounded husky, heavy with grief, and Bree's ears rang with a keening wail.

"When your mother died," Sibeal began, "the Council all but died with her. We lost our two elders. I was the youngest, and the only one to survive."

Muffled voices throbbed through Bree's awareness. Then a woman called out, "No! You don't have to do this," as another whispered, "Be careful." She could hear footsteps resounding against the steady whine of the rain, until a woman's scream pierced through it all. Bree pressed her eyes closed against the shrill intrusion. When she opened her eyes again, Sibeal was watching her.

"Bríde's death hit me hard. We were very close, your mother and I." Tears shone in Sibeal's eyes. "Coupled with the loss of my sister warriors... Well... It took me a few years before I could think about reforming the Council." Sibeal huffed. "And that was anything but easy. Ailene was still a girl, far too young to take her place. And Cara..." She turned toward the red-haired woman beside her, shook her head and chuckled. "Cara refused to leave her sanctuary."

Shrugging her right shoulder, Cara offered Bree a lopsided grin.

"What changed your mind?" Emily asked, her gaze firmly focused on the graying, redheaded warrior.

Cara turned and gestured to the woman on her right. "Ailene."

Ailene smiled.

"When she came of age, I realized the Council could function again."

Sibeal heaved a deep sigh, shifting restlessly in her seat. "Which brings us to the reason for our visit."

She paused. Spreading her hands before her, palms upward, Sibeal searched them as if for support. Cara drew breath to speak, but Sibeal placed a hand on her thigh and silenced her with a shake of her head. Then, palms again facing upward, she lifted her gaze to Bree.

Bree gasped. A tidal wave of sorrow poured over her, pummeling her and pulling her downward. Dropping her gaze, she gripped the arms of her chair and dug in her nails, attempting to upright herself. But the sorrow wailed on, seeped into her.

No, Bree told herself, *this is not your own. Let this go. Step out of the connection. Let this go.*

She could not.

Images pounded through her... Sibeal and Bríde laughing as young girls, spinning wool... Sibeal and Bríde standing in the family grove, gazing up at the moon... Sibeal and Bríde watching their husbands run on the rugby field... Sibeal kneeling at the waters edge, releasing a handful of Bríde's ashes into the running stream... Sibeal waiting outside the hospital as Emily carried Bree out to safety.

Bree looked up and found herself held in Sibeal's gaze again. *She knows what she is doing. She is sending me these images, rather than speak it again.*

"I am so sorry, Bree" Sibeal's voice trembled. "I... I knew he was against you. I knew he had turned against the Old Ways. I saw him embracing the new religion, heard him speaking of our tradition as evil. I knew he was planning... planning to hurt you. He saw you as some form of the Devil... as Satan incarnate, but I... I just couldn't believe it... I just couldn't..."

Sibeal closed her eyes and shook her head slowly. "You were so young. I tried to keep an eye on you, to honor my promise to your mother. But I was the only one left...the only one..." Tears spilled silently from Sibeal's eyes. "I failed to protect you, like I failed your mother." Opening her eyes, she set her shoulders. "It won't happen again."

She knows the truth, Bree realized. Her breath caught at her sides as her heart raced. "But why... Why would he...?"

Sibeal just shook her head.

Emily sighed. "It started in Ireland."

Bree turned to find her foster-mother staring into the past, her eyes glazed with memory.

"He climbed Croagh Patrick – the site of his namesake's first church in Ireland – and spent three days and nights there, without shelter, food or water. He said Patrick had called to him in a dream, had told him to climb his mountain. He believed Patrick was waiting for him there."

Emily's voice trailed to silence. Bree wanted to reach out, to shake her aunt until she finished the story. She gripped the arms of her chair to keep her hands occupied.

Emily bowed her head. "Well, you know what the Irish say about people who sleep out on the hills. It proved true for Patrick. He was never the same after that. He became obsessed, studying the life and teachings of his namesake. He started going to church, studying the Bible and saying Catholic prayers. He ranted endlessly about Patrick driving the snakes out of Ireland." Emily turned her now-clear gaze to Bree. "And he hated your mother. After she died, his hatred turned on you."

"And I did nothing." Sibeal dropped her head into her hands as tears spilled onto the floor. "I did nothing."

"*We* did nothing," Cara amended, moving her hand to caress her friend's back tenderly. "It was *our* fault, not yours alone."

Bree watched Sibeal's silver plait slip across her back and down her shaking shoulders. It hung there, swinging like a pendulum, and Bree found herself staring at it. With each small arc, the keening wail returned, growing slowly to fill her ears, then ripping through her awareness. The haunting, screech-like sound sent shivers aching through her body, and she shook herself, trying to break free from the eerie cry.

Ailene cleared her throat and leaned forward, gaining a clear view of the older woman seated at the other end of the couch. "That was two years before my initiation into the Council. Without Cara, Sibeal, there was nothing you could do. You were entirely alone."

Cara nodded. "We've come a long way since then."

"*I've* come a long way since then." Ailene grimaced and looked at the woman beside her. "But, it is kind of you not to single me out." She sighed and turned to look Bree directly in the eyes. "The point is – Cousine, you are no longer alone."

JENNIFER LYNN

CHAPTER THIRTY-NINE

Bree stood in the guest bedroom of Rose's house, watching the rain play on the windows. *Love, Love, Love,* the raindrops called. Inhaling deeply, Bree drank in that song, let that Love flow through her.

Her body thrummed, but she was empty. Hollow. All she had learned from her cousines had drained her completely.

Looking around, Bree sighed. *I belonged here once.* But that was long ago. Before she had chosen to love a woman. Before her Otherworldly gifts had fully awakened. Before she had become a *Bean feasa,* a healer, a soul midwife. Before she had discovered who she was.

She could forgive them now, even her uncle. She could bless the past, let it go and let herself heal.

I choose to embrace healing. I choose to trust in Love.

A knock rapped softly behind her. Bree turned to see Emily standing in the open doorway.

"That was a lot for one night. I wanted to be sure you were okay."

Bree sighed, letting her head and shoulders droop. "I'm okay." She nodded, lifting her gaze to look at her aunt.

Emily's eyes narrowed slightly, looking more deeply, seeking the Truth in her niece's energetic field. The gesture was so familiar that Bree chuckled softly.

"Really." Bree nodded. "Now the hurt can heal."

Bree wanted to reassure her aunt, but how? What could she say to let Love flow again? Words surfaced from her childhood.

"The pathway to healing..." Bree began.

Emily smiled. She had taught Bree that mantra. Joining her niece in the recitation, the two women finished it together. "The pathway to healing shines brightest in the light of Truth."

They stood in silence, wise woman with wise woman.

Emily had raised Bree, had tutored Bree in the ebbings and flowings of the Otherworld, had helped Bree recognize the calling to awaken. Now, in her own way, Bree had done the same for Emily. She had helped her aunt awaken to a deeper understanding of the sacred teachings of their family's tradition, and had mid-wifed her aunt's initiation into the next phase of her soul's becoming. Through it all, Love had shown them the way.

Outside the window, the rain sang its gentle reminder... *Love, Love, Love...*

Bree picked up the flannel shirt she had set down earlier, refolded it and placed it in her suitcase. Emily stood watching her pack.

"Will you head back to Saint Louis, then?"

Bree shook her head. "Not yet." Images rushed through her... Bree and Gwen laughing in Forest Park... Bree and Gwen sipping coffee under the oak trees... Bree and Gwen cooking dinner in their kitchen... "That was our city, mine and Gwen's. I'm not sure I am ready to see it without her."

Emily nodded. "Where will you go?"

Bree shrugged. "Back to Ireland. Back to the cottage."

Emily smiled broadly. "Your mother loved that cottage. I was so glad she left it to you. How long will you stay?"

Bree picked up a pair of jeans from the pile of freshly washed clothes on the bed. After folding them, she placed them in her suitcase.

"Until the path forward shines clearly for me again."

Her favorite dragon tee shirt remained unfolded on the bed. Bree picked it up and smiled. She had worn that shirt the night Fiona followed Bríghid's call to the grove. She shook it out before folding it. After placing it in her suitcase, Bree turned back toward Emily.

"Will you do something for me, foster-mother?"

Emily nodded, tears welling in her eyes. "If I may."

Bree sighed. "Teach Fiona well."

Emily shook her head and furrowed her brow. "Fiona?"

"Fiona." Bree turned back to the bed and zipped her suitcase closed.

"You know," Emily hesitated, "you are welcome to stay here. We could teach her together…"

Bree paused. *I choose to embrace healing. I choose to trust in Love.*

"Thank you, foster-mother." Bree smiled. "But, you know very well, this is not my home anymore."

Emily nodded. "I know. But I had to ask the question."

CHAPTER FORTY

Bree MacLeod sat watching her Salmon Ally glide through the school of brass salmon swimming endlessly along the floor of Seattle-Tacoma International Airport. Boarding pass in hand, she gazed softly, chuckling as her Ally darted in and out amongst the permanently hovering fish.

At least Salmon is enjoying this place.

As if in reply, her Ally paused, shifted to face Bree and winked.

"Time to go home, Raven Child." Salmon nodded, turned upstream and swam away, disappearing into the Otherworld.

Bree checked her boarding pass before tucking it into the pocket of her messenger bag. Thirty minutes. In thirty minutes she would board a flight to Newark, where she would catch another flight to Shannon. This time tomorrow she would be back in Ireland.

You are correct, Salmon, Bree smiled. *Time to go home.*

Home. The word made Bree frown. Where exactly was her home?

Time was Seattle had been her home. But she had left, had cultivated a new way of living and being, and learned to thrive in another place, in another way. While she was grateful to be reunited with her family, here, now, she knew for certain that Seattle was no longer home.

Cape Breton then, she pondered.

After her mother's death plunged her father into unspeakable grief, he had left Bree in Emily's care and returned to his home in Cape Breton. Over the years Bree had spent time with him and their relatives there. She loved the smell of the salt air and the wail of the bagpipes singing the sun to rest over St. Anns Bay. The view from MacLeod's Point made her heart sigh. But was it home?

In a way, Saint Louis had become her home. She had an apartment, a circle of friends, and kept most of her belongings there. Her business address was Clayton, a city in the Saint Louis metropolitan area, although she could – and often did – work from almost any physical location. After all, the Otherworld is everywhere.

But, Saint Louis had been *their* home, the city of Bree and Gwen. Now that Gwen was gone, did she still want to make a life there?

And then there was Ireland.

The stone and thatch cottage she inherited from her mother was the only place Bree truly knew peace. She could still remember the first time her feet had touched the *machair*, the soil of Éireann's Blessed Isle. Breaking free of the din of Dublin, Bree had stripped off her shoes and walked barefoot upon Mother Éireann.

"I am here," Bree had whispered.

The response had flowed gently, a loving embrace that enfolded Bree from her feet to her head, then draped gently around her shoulders.

Wrapped in Éireann's blessing, all the noise had simply stopped. The aching, the yearning that had pursued and haunted Bree throughout this lifetime simply vanished. Bathed in peace, Bree heard Mother Éireann whisper for the first time…

"…*Fáilte abhaile… Welcome home.*"

Ireland, Saint Louis, Cape Breton, Seattle… all of these places offered a *home* for Bree.

But what is a home, Bree wondered. What did the word "home" mean to her anymore? Was it a physical place? Was a home something you belonged to by birth? Something you were born to be? Or could it be a way of being?

"Good morning, ladies and gentlemen. In just a few minutes, we will begin boarding United flight 1695 to Newark, New Jersey…"

The airline attendant's voice blared harshly from the loudspeaker, jostling Bree energetically. She shifted physically in her seat to release the discomfort, upsetting the book in her lap in the process. Picking it up, a red rose, dried and pressed, slipped into view.

Bree smiled. Rose had gifted Bree the flower this morning. Exchanging hugs at the airport departures curb, Rose had thanked her for coming. Bree had smiled and answered honestly.

"I had to come. It was the right thing, for everyone."

Rose had nodded, her gaze drifting briefly. "Bree…"

Rose had hesitated, her energy bristling and uncomfortable. Bree could sense the unspoken question. So, she had simply waited, welcoming her cousine's inquiry.

"Bree, why didn't you mention Gwen's passing?"

Sighing gustily, Bree shook her head. "At first I couldn't… I just couldn't. Then…" Bree shifted her gaze to look directly into her cousine's eyes. "Well… so much time had passed…"

They stood in silence a while, Rose scanning Bree's energetic field, considering her response. With a nod of understanding, Rose stepped forward and drew Bree into a parting hug. Stepping back, Rose started toward the car, then paused. Love humming throughout her energetic body, Rose had turned to face Bree.

"This week I witnessed the beauty of rebirth. A woman re-awakened within my mother the ability to love. You know, another woman might be able to do the same for you."

Quietly, Bree had reminded herself of her recent choice. *I choose to embrace healing. I choose to trust in Love.* Leaning into that trust, Bree allowed herself to receive fully the Love flowing from her cousine. She breathed it in, let it flow to the very depths of her. The whisper her heart and soul had offered in reply surprised her.

"It isn't that simple."

Rose had nodded. Taking Bree's hand, Rose had pressed the flower into her cousine's palm.

"Still, I hope you can let go of Gwen enough to find out. You know, she would want that for you, too."

Bree picked the rose out from between the pages of her book. Resting in her hand, the rose hummed and thrummed of Love. Through the noise of the airport, Bree could hear that Love singing to her.

Then another song rippled through her awareness, drawing her attention to her messenger bag. With Love still singing to her, Bree pulled out her ringing telephone and read the number on the display.

"He loves you."

Bree lifted her gaze from the telephone. There, but not entirely, the ghostly image of a woman sat in the next seat gazing tenderly at Bree.

Gwen, Bree whispered.

The woman smiled warmly.

Bree's telephone sang out again, but Bree just sat there. Bathed in the song of Love, her telephone in her hand, she stared at the ghostly image of Gwen.

"You really should answer it."

Bree knew sorrow danced in her eyes. To her surprise, she felt no tears rise or fall.

For a third time Bree's telephone sang its song, and the ghostly image of Gwen smiled.

"He loves you. Answer it. Answer it, with my blessing."

Gwen rose and stood before Bree. *"Trust in Love again,"* Gwen whispered, then she turned and disappeared with the swimming salmon into the Otherworld.

Bree drew in a deep, steadying breath. *I choose to trust in Love. I choose to trust in Love. I choose to trust in Love.* Lifting the telephone to her ear, Bree answered the call.

"Hello…"

EPILOGUE

"How long will you be in Scotland?"

Bree sat on the bed in the cottage her mother had left to her in Ireland. An open suitcase rested, half full, beside her. She pulled restlessly at a pair of wool socks waiting to be packed.

"Bree? Did I lose you?" Fergus Sinclair called through the telephone.

Bree sighed. "No, I'm still here."

"How long will you be in Scotland?" Fergus asked again.

Bree could hear the yearning in his voice. It ached, pulsing through her like a heartbeat. "I don't know exactly."

She was avoiding him, and she knew it.

They had been friends for several years and had grown quite close over the last three. Fergus was kind, supportive and encouraging, always offering a laugh when Bree needed it most. When Gwen passed and Bree fell to pieces, Fergus had been there for her. He had brought food and sat with her, making sure she ate at least two meals a day. Understanding her connection to the land, he had dragged her out of bed and walked her to her favorite park, so she could sit beneath the oak trees. And, when Bree could not tolerate idle chatter, he had sat beside her in silence.

Fergus hesitated. "I was hoping you might come home soon."

"Home," Bree chuckled. "You mean, back to Saint Louis."

"Well, yeah."

He loved her.

Gwen was right, Bree admitted, picking at the wool socks beside her.

He had never said as much, but Bree now knew it was true. The thought sent heat pulsating through her. Her energy body tingled as her heart raced, and she scowled.

Strange, she frowned. *Could I possibly love him, too?*

GLOSSARY
IRISH PHRASES AND PRONUNCIATIONS

The sounds of the English language differ from those of the Irish. The pronunciations listed here are attempts at phonetic renderings of Irish sounds. Please know that these are approximations only, a starting point for those daring enough to try.

A stór... dearest, my dear, darling. Used to refer to a cherished family member or loved one. Pronounced "uh store."

Aes Dána... the Gifted, those blessed by the goddess Dánu / Dána and imbued with Otherworldly skills. Pronounced "ace donna."

Ailene... an Irish girl's name. Derived from the Irish word *ail*, meaning *noble*. Pronounced "ay-len-uh."

Airds... the directions of the Celtic Wheel: north, east, south, west and center. Pronounced like "arts" but with "air" in place of "ar"... "air-ts."

Anam cara... soul friends. Pronounced "on-um car-uh."

Bean Feasa... wise woman, shaman, walker between the worlds. Pronounced "bahn fah-sah."

Beannachtaí... blessings. Pronounced "bahn-nach-tee," with the "nach" aspirated in the throat.

Beannachtaí, a stór... Blessings, dearest. Pronounced "bahn-nach-tee a store."

Beannachtaí, mo Ghrá... Blessings, my love. Pronounced "bahn-nach-tee moe hraw."

Beannachtaí, mo leanbh... Blessings, my child. Pronounced "bahn-nach-tee moe lah-nuv."

Bríde... a variation of the name Bríghid. Pronounced "bree-je."

Brígh... a variation of the name Bríghid. Pronounced "bree-he," with the "he" as a slight aspiration in the throat at the end.

Bríghid... the Celtic goddess of the forge, smithcraft, poetry, midwifing and the keeper of the Sacred Flame. Pronounced "bree-hid" or "bree-git."

Caol Ina... a single malt scotch from the Scottish Hebrides. Pronounced "kale eena."

Cara... an Irish girl's name. *Cara* in Irish means *friend*. Pronounced "car-uh."

Chiya... although not actually Irish, the word deserves explanation. First encountered in Marion Zimmer Bradley's *Darkover* series, the term has stayed in my vocabulary. The closest translation is *dearest*, *dear heart* or *beloved*. Pronounced "chee-yuh" or "shee-yuh."

Ciara... an Irish girl's name. From the Irish word *ciar*, meaning *dark*. It implies a dark-haired, dark-eyed female. Pronounced "key-are-uh."

Éireann... Ireland. Also the name of one of the three mother goddesses of Ireland. Pronounced "erin."

Fáilte abhaile... Welcome home. Pronounced "fall-chuh a-wall-ye."

Fáth Fíth... an incantation chanted to cast a cloak of invisibility upon someone. Pronounced "faw fee."

Fiona... an Irish girl's name, meaning "Bright" or "Fair one". Pronounced "fee-oh-na."

Go raibh mille maith agaibh... Thank you (formal). Pronounced "go rev meal-uh my uh-give."

Machair... the soil, the earth of Ireland. Pronounced "ma-hair."

Mo Ghrá... my love. Pronounced "moe hraw."

Mo leanbh... my child. Pronounced "moe lah-nuv."

Sibeal... an Irish girl's name. A Gaelic version of the Hebrew Elisheba and the English Sybil, meaning "God is my oath." Pronounced "She-bell."

the Sídhe... also called the People of Peace and the Ancient Ones. The *Sídhe* are the ancient guardians of and the in dwelling spirits of the land. *Sídhe* is pronounced "she."

Sin é... literally, "It is". Used as the equivalent of "Amen" or "So mote it be". Pronounced "shin-a," with the "a" sounding long, as in "hay," but without the "h" sound.

ACKNOWLEDGEMENTS

Nine years ago I heard Bree MacLeod whispering for the first time. Her story immediately called to me. But, a poet at heart, I was reluctant to write a tale of fiction. I am deeply grateful that I did. Thank you Bree, for your patience, then and now.

Many people appeared at just the right moment along this journey of Love. Their contributions and support took many forms, from words of encouragement to insightful conversations and simple smiles. To all of you, thank you.

I am especially grateful to Ravenswood Publishing and Kitty Bullard for welcoming Bree and her story to their family of books.

Heartfelt gratitude to Dawn Leslie Lenz for a beautiful cover befitting Bree's story and quiet confidence in a moment of need.

And a smile of gentle thanks to my photographer, Teofilo (Ted) Moreno of MorenoGallery.com.

Thanks also to the fabulous writing community of Saint Louis, Missouri. From the Writers' Guild to the poetry slams, my heart smiles to live enfolded in your celebration of the Bardic Arts. I must salute two fabulous writing groups. To the (Un)Stable Writers – Ben Moeller-Gaa, Dawn Leslie Lenz, Autumn Rinaldi and friends – thanks for asking excellent questions and supporting my disappearances to spend quality time with Bree. To my critique group partners – Brad R. Cook, Cole Gibsen and TWFendley – thanks for welcoming a newbie.

I must also honor my courageous Beta readers, Theresa Schnellmann, Faye Schrater, Tom Cowan, Tim Altepeter and Stefanie Otterson. Your encouragement and your honesty freed Bree's voice to sing more clearly.

This book embodies twenty-five years of mystical practice and study. Murmuring through its pages are the voices of many teachers from my journeys in the Otherworld as well as This World, including Tom Cowan, Caitlín Matthews, Geo Cameron, Karl Schlotterbeck, Frank MacEowen and Philip Carr-Gomm. Words cannot express my gratitude for you all. Special thanks and deep honor to my Council of Allies, Mother Brighid and the Sacred Three. Thank you for your Love, your Grace, for everything. Blessed is the Sacred Conversation.

And to Tim Altepeter, who always asked after Bree, brought countless almond milk steamers to warm the writing process, and believed unswervingly in both Bree and me, thank you for being here. *This is Love... a stór.*

Beannachtaí... Blessings...

ABOUT THE AUTHOR

Jennifer Lynn is a soul midwife, a modern-day mystic and a shamanic practitioner specializing in Celtic mystical techniques and practices. During twenty-plus years of training and experience, she has studied extensively with Tom Cowan, Caitlín Matthews, the Invisible Druid Order, the Order of Bards Ovates and Druids, the Foundation for Shamanic Studies as well as with mystical practitioners internationally.

An award-winning, published poet, Jennifer gives voice to her Bardic craft through poetry and prose. Her writings explore the rhythms of life while honoring the Goddess and the Sacred Conversation. Dance through the moon turnings with Jennifer – read her blog at:

www.ThroughShamansEyes.wordpress.com

Jennifer is also a Chinese medicine practitioner and a Minister of the Circle of the Sacred Earth, a church of animism fostering shamanic principles and practices. She currently resides in Saint Louis, Missouri, under the Fleur-de-Lys, nestled amongst the waters and the oak trees.

Made in the USA
Lexington, KY
16 May 2017